b,

Book,

and Me

Also by
Kim Sagwa

Mina

b, Book, and Me

Kim Sagwa

Translated from Korean by
Sunhee Jeong

TWO LINES
PRESS

Originally published as: 나b책 by Kim Sagwa
Copyright © 2011 by Kim Sagwa
Originally published in Korea by Changbi Publishers, Inc.
English Edition is published in arrangement with Changbi Publishers, Inc.

Translation © 2020 by Sunhee Jeong

Two Lines Press
582 Market Street, Suite 700, San Francisco, CA 94104
www.twolinespress.com

ISBN 978-1-931883-96-2

Names: Kim Sagwa, author. | Jeong, Sunhee, translator.
Title: b, Book, and Me / by Kim Sagwa; translated by Sunhee Jeong.
Description: English edition. | San Francisco : Two Lines Press, [2020] |
"Originally published in Korea by Changbi Publishers, Inc., © 2011." |
Summary: When b and Rang's friendship ends they are completely alone until a
mysterious man, Book, introduces them to the part of town where lunatics live--the
End. Identifiers: LCCN 2019025997 | ISBN 9781931883962 (paperback)
Subjects: CYAC: Best friends--Fiction. | Friendship--Fiction. |
Schools--Fiction. | Bullying--Fiction. | Family problems--Fiction. |
Eccentrics and eccentricities--Fiction. | Korea--Fiction.
Classification: LCC PZ7.1.S58367 Baaf 2020 | DDC [Fic]--dc23
LC record available at https://lccn.loc.gov/2019025997

Cover design by Gabriele Wilson
Cover photo by Miguel Sobreira / Millennium Images, UK
Typeset by Jessica Sevey

Printed in the United States of America

1 3 5 7 9 10 8 6 4 2

This book is published with the support of the Literature Translation
Institute of Korea (LTI Korea) and is supported in part by an award
from the National Endowment for the Arts.

A Seaside City

A face as stiff as a boulder, stiff with boredom—
that's the face of an adult.

Adults don't think about the ocean
even when they watch it.

Their minds are full of other things.

It's very depressing to think
that someday I, too, will be an adult.

1

We lived on the coast.

2

As I stood at the end of the breakwater, my body swayed against a gust of wind. When I looked out over the ocean, the waves filled my eyes. They pushed in and died out, from left to right, then from the left again, making white foam. The foam looked like a sponge or little snowballs. It felt good to watch the small white bubbles disappear when they touched my skin. That's why I came to the breakwater every day. Even on extremely cold or extremely hot days. Sometimes a strong gust of wind would push me one step, no, two steps to the right. But it didn't scare me. The frothy waves reminded me of winter. I thought about snow, which I've never actually seen, and all at once, I would be standing in the middle of a snowy winter field. The blue ocean would completely transform into a white field of snow. Winter tumbling over the ground. If I lay flat on my stomach, it would spill over my back. It tumbled and tumbled, then jumped into the waves to melt away without a trace. I'd stand still, my swaying body tight, and etch the winter field onto my memory.

Besides me, the breakwater was always teeming with tanned boys. I knew them very well. We all went to the same school, since there was only one school in our city, and *that's* because we lived in a very small city. The boys would stand at the tip of the breakwater with their arms crossed, looking silently down at the water, and then, all of a sudden, they'd jump in. A wet head would pop up, grinning happily. Skinny muscular arms would plow through the water and climb back up the breakwater. The boys thumped each other's soaked backs. They laughed and yelled, sang songs and danced. When they shook their heads, drops of water fell on their shoulders, sparkling in the blinding-white sunlight.

One day, I was passing by the noisy group of boys, and one of them, grinning, playfully yanked my hair. I held my bag tightly in both arms and walked faster. Then the boy swore and began to chase me. Frightened, I picked up a stone and threw it. The stone hit him, gashing his forehead. He stared at me, eyes wide with surprise as red blood smeared down his forehead. The other kids started yelling, screaming, *ii ii,* like angry monkeys. I hunched my back, clasping my bag even more tightly and picking up my pace. The boys continued, *ii, ii.* I was scared, but they didn't do anything except make monkey noises. Anyway, after that, no one yanked my hair again. But it was even worse: when I passed the boys, they hunched their shoulders and whispered among themselves. They didn't laugh or dance. I missed watching them laugh and dance and jump into the ocean.

I opened my bag and peered inside. Inside was my pencil case, some notebooks, and a mirror. I took out the mirror and held it up to my face. The mirror didn't reflect any light. I held it to the sun. It shone with light. The boys stopped whispering and stared at me. Still holding out the mirror, I walked. I walked faster and faster. I tried to smile, but couldn't.

3

Sometimes, the dads who took their boats out to sea didn't return. Morning came with its rising sun, then night came again, shining with stars, but the dads didn't return. People, sobbing and tearing their hair out, came to the beach. They waited. They waited a long time. But nothing happened. The sun sparkled and the stars shone. The ocean rocked from the left to the right. Everything was the same. No one came back.

Some days, a brave child would swim far out and wouldn't return. Then the brave child's mother would come, wailing, staggering along the sandy shore. If she was lucky, a body would be pushed back onto the shore. When that happened, the wind stopped blowing and the waves stopped swaying. People gathered around the body. The other children would stand far back from the breakwater and stare, silent.

Sometimes, a lonely person walked right into the ocean. It was always at night, and it was always someone from a faraway place we'd never heard of. A few days later, people would arrive in their cars, carrying the person's photograph, and go into Highway Grocery. But the old lady who owned Highway Grocery was too old to remember anything. The sun sparkled more brightly than ever, and so did the ocean. The boys jumped into the water, and I lay on my stomach at the edge of the breakwater. In the end, no one came back. Everything stayed the same.

4

It was noon. The sky was completely dark and hushed rain fell. I had taken off all my clothes and was standing at the end of the deserted breakwater, staring into the ocean. The waves whirled violently, creating foam that was bigger than my body. Overall, the ocean seemed to be extremely busy, so I couldn't talk to it. But standing still and not saying anything is boring. I got bored and put my clothes back on. My clothes were wet, like my body. I hugged my bag and started to walk away from the breakwater. The rain fell more heavily. The wind whirled around and around, from left to right, then from the left again. I shook and swayed along with it. The sky was a huge ocean, and it poured itself down on my head. The ocean poured down on the ocean. The sandy beach and roads were oceans as well. The rain fell even more strongly. A huge wave reached over the breakwater and yanked at my ankle. Startled, I began to cry, and then my eyes were the ocean as well. My cheeks, my neck, my shoulders, and my belly button all became the ocean. Everything was the ocean. Everything was the same. *That means we're on the same side. I'm on the same side as the waves, the sky, the earth, the ocean.* Nothing was scary if I thought of it that way. I was the waves, I was the earth, and I was water. I lifted my arms high into the air, and let my bag drop to the ground. The falling rain and me, the waves and the ocean and me, the earth and water and me, we were all one. The rain grew stronger, so I grew stronger. We all grew stronger together. Eventually, I became so strong that I forgot who I was. I forgot what I was doing and where I was going. Without a thought for my bag, I started walking.

Without thinking about my bag.

Without thinking.

Without thinking about all that was bad.

Without thinking.

Without thinking.

I opened my closed eyes. Rain ran down my entire body. I was happy. I was happy.

5

I got into trouble with my mom.

I also got a cold, a new bag, pencil case, and mirror.

7

6

The city was located east of the ocean. Everybody who lived there was pretty much the same. We all went to the same school, watched movies at the same movie theater, and ate hamburgers at the same burger place. We all dreamed the same dream—we didn't dream at all. We just swayed like the waves, back and forth, back and forth, ending up in the same place we were before. Except there was one kid who wanted to be a fish. That's b, sitting right next to me. "Then you can just go into the water and stay there," said b. "You can stay there forever. You don't have to pay rent. You don't have to go grocery shopping. You don't even have to work or go to school. You won't need money. You can be poor," said b, who was poor.

"I want to go into the water and never come out."

b reached down and brushed the sand off her knees.

I waited for b to start talking again.

"I want to be a fish."

That's all b said.

But in my opinion, it wouldn't be that easy. "Being a fish," I said, "means that you have scales all over you." I put my palms together and stretched them out toward b. "It means that your body is flat. It means that you have fins and gills, that your legs disappear." I tightened my fists and shook. "You'd be ugly. Is that what you want? Are you into that?"

"Yeah, I am."

b was resolute.

"I'll go into the water and I'll never come back out."

We were sitting on the sand. The ocean glittered, reflecting the sunlight. It was a really splendid Friday afternoon in the middle of spring. But there weren't any slim women in flowery bikinis, or well-tanned men hitting on them. You couldn't find people like that here, not even in the summer. Because our city is dull. "In Seoul," Glasses once said, "you can get a TV as big as fifteen of the TVs in the classroom put together. But it's even thinner than my workbook." Glasses was our class president. He was talking about Seoul again. But we all knew as little about Seoul as we did about how to turn into a fish. Actually, turning into a fish sounded more feasible than living in Seoul. Glasses wanted to live in Seoul, so he worked feverishly on his workbook through his thick glasses. I thought Glasses' parents were pretty impressive if they'd named him Glasses knowing he'd wear glasses and study hard. Glasses was sitting with us on the sand, but instead of just wasting time like we were, he was solving problems in his workbook. Glasses' aunt, who lived in Seoul, had bought him the book. Supposedly, all smart students in Seoul use that brand to study. Glasses had one for every subject. He particularly liked the math one, which could be why he was very good at math. We called Glasses the King of Math.

Glasses, the King of Math, sat on the sand, finding the length of side *a* for an unknown figure. I was imagining the television screen supposedly sold in Seoul, as big as fifteen of the classroom television sets put together. I imagined myself watching the screen. Wouldn't my neck hurt? I'd have to watch it from far away. But if you sat far away, wouldn't the screen seem smaller? Then why would you barley tea, which was about ten minutes. We placed stickers that said "Quality Guaranteed—Fisheries Cooperative Association" on the plastic bags. The lady lit a cigarette and then went outside. She sat on a plastic chair outside the door, smoking and watching the ocean. We didn't know anything about her. We weren't curious to know, either. And she knew that. Nobody was curious about her, which meant that she didn't have anyone to talk to. Instead, she quietly made barley tea, distributed clam meat into plastic bags, and smoked cigarettes. Just like the ocean and the forest, the old lady, without a word, got older every day.

8

A little walk from Highway Grocery took us to an old alley. The alleyway, which was dry and crisp with sunlight, was so quiet I could hear the sound of b's breathing. We walked in silence. Occasionally we changed directions, or moved slightly to the side to avoid cars. As we walked, the city slowly came into view. Reluctant to leave the ocean, I looked back several times. The ocean was slowly falling out of sight. It eventually disappeared completely, once the sandy coast and the hills and the forests that covered the hills could no longer be seen; once the wind didn't smell of sand, dust, and salt, we were in the city. Being in the city felt strange. As if I were trapped in a mirror. No matter where I looked, I was the only one there. Of course, I was still with b. We were even holding hands. But I could no longer see her, nor hear her, nor feel her. It was very scary and strange.

9

The city we lived in was ridiculous, because it was a city that imitated Seoul. But the more it imitated Seoul, the more it became... not Seoul and foolish. People bought cars from Seoul Motors and ate at Seoul Kitchen. They bought glasses from Seoul Eyewear and went on trips through Seoul Tours. We all knew how absurd it was. But we didn't know how to do anything that wasn't absurd. The determined ones, the ones who were set against absurdity, left the city and went to the real Seoul. Like how Glasses will leave someday. Or like how his aunt had already left.

Seoul Tours sold three-day packaged trips to Seoul, which my school bought every year for our annual field trip. On the first day of the trip, we all arrived at Seoul Station early in the morning. Seoul Station was big, white, and new. It was so big that our whole city could have fit inside of it. We waited for a native Seoul tour guide, who was supposedly born in Seoul and knew it very well. Her name was Sara. While waiting for Sara, we ate American bread laden with sugar and watched the sophisticated Seoul people. They all stared straight ahead and walked quickly with stern faces. Sara was ten minutes late, but didn't apologize. She had permed hair that was dyed brown and looked sophisticated, like Seoul. The boys in my class were already blushing, having fallen in love with her. Sara took us to the center of Seoul. There was a museum, a movie theater, and the royal palace. It was evening by the time we finished visiting them. On the second day, we went to Myeong-dong, a department store, the 63 Building, and the Han River.

always saying. "If you get lost, you'll end up in the End. Lots of children get lost, wander into the End, and never come out," Grandma said. Grandma said that the End was where the crooks, thieves, prostitutes, orphans, murderers, and insane people lived. All I knew about those types of people was what I saw in movies or read in comic books. Even in movies or comics, they lived in places like the End. Everyone drank liquor instead of water and ate rotten food instead of vegetables, and no one went to school or to work. Corpses lay in the streets, and mice and cockroaches scuttled through the houses. I once saw a movie on television in which the main character, looking for the villain, went to a place like the End. The streets were dark and wet, and crazy people in torn clothes came up to him. I was afraid and shook Grandma to wake her up, though she had been sound asleep. She asked what was wrong and I pointed to the TV, asking if the End that Grandma talked about was as terrible as that. Grandma didn't even glance at the television, replying right away that it was.

When I was sick or lonely, I always dreamed about going to the End. In my dream, b lived there, because she was turning into a fish. If the people in the city saw b turning into a fish, they'd report her to the police or shut her up in a zoo, but that didn't happen in the End. People there weren't bothered by something like that. *I'm turning into a fish. I need a house*, b would say, scratching at her scales. A man would reply, *Is that so? I know someone who's turning into a plate…* and he'd get her a room to stay in. So b—turning into a fish—lived next door to a person who was turning into a plate. When I went to visit b, she had pulled a blanket over herself. I said, *Hi*, and she crawled out from under it. b's chest was covered with scales, and in the light they sparkled in all the colors of the rainbow. *Feel it*, said b. I felt it. Her chest was as cold as ice. b wasn't going to leave that room until she'd completely changed. *When I'm finished turning into a fish,* b said, scratching at her neck, *put me in the ocean.* b's shorter and thicker neck had faint, crimson lines—she was growing gills. b held my hand. Her fingers had shrunk. *You have to come here every day to see whether I've finished turning into a fish or not. Or else I might die.* Then she started making noises like air escaping, *shii, shii.* The shape of her face sharpened. Her eyes grew apart. I took a few steps backward. b's face shined silvery. I screamed. I always woke up from the dream at that moment. Then I'd run to Grandma, crying. Grandma wouldn't wake up, but it was warm in her arms, and scale-free. "Grandma," I'd whisper, "I'm not going to turn into a fish. I'm not going to be anything." And then I'd hug Grandma's arm tightly and close my eyes. Soon I'd fall into a dreamless sleep.

11

Sometimes I did well on tests; sometimes I didn't. Sometimes I studied hard; sometimes I didn't study at all. Sometimes I did all my homework; sometimes I didn't do any of it. My mom and dad didn't care either way. Whether I finished my homework a hundred times in a row, or skipped it a hundred times in a row, my mom and dad didn't care. They were constantly frowning, busy with other stuff. When they were home, they were usually asleep. Occasionally, if they were just sitting, not doing anything, they would say, *I'm tired, go away.* So I was angry. I was angry and I wanted to bring my mom the hundred pieces of homework I hadn't done and ask her, *Why did you have me in the first place?* But in the end I didn't. I decided not to care about my parents either. No, I decided to pretend not to care. Instead I'd go to Grandma. When I lay down on Grandma's lap and closed my eyes, she told me exciting stories. She talked about things I didn't know anything about, like the End and hunger and war. Grandma was getting gradually younger. She liked eating candy, and took clothes out of the drawers to refold them a hundred times a day. She kept forgetting to eat and got angry at us. But when she told me stories, Grandma didn't seem like a child. She remembered everything and told them superbly.

Through the window in my room on the second floor, I could see two-story houses that looked exactly like our house. At night, cross signs lit up on top of the houses. Against their glow, the stars dimmed. I'd close my window, lie on my bed, and either do or not do my homework. When I got hungry, Grandma called out to me. Most of the time, I lay still on my bed instead of doing my homework. I didn't read or listen to music or think about boys I liked. Time didn't seem to flow at all, as though I was in a lukewarm puddle. Everything was quiet and still, like air in a closed room. That was my world. I liked it.

The teachers at school had never liked me, particularly my homeroom teacher, because I would work hard for a while, and then not at all. But that spring, the boys in class began to hate me as well. They didn't have a reason. And the teachers who hated me pretended not to notice. One day, I fell flat on my face in the schoolyard, because a boy had punched me. I fell to the ground then rolled over. The boy's friends laughed hard. Blood was coming out of my nose, and I could see the sky clearly. About ten boys were looking down at me, their faces seeming to think hard about what to do with me. I continued to watch the sky. The boys continued to stare at me. When I turned my head to the side, I saw in the distance, between the legs of the boys, my homeroom teacher carrying a parasol with flowers on it. The flowers were lilies. I knew that my teacher saw me but that she was pretending she didn't. Of course, the boys knew it as well. So then I pretended with them. We all pretended. A boy kicked at me. I rolled to the right. Then I rolled to the left, then back to the right again. As I rolled, it occurred to me that it was everyone who was watching. That is: the sky, the school, my teacher, Glasses, b, Grandma, my dad, my mom—they were all watching me, but they all pretended not to. That thought made me sad. But I held back the tears with all my strength. Then I stopped rolling and opened my eyes…to see b.

b, holding a recorder in each hand, was running toward the boys, brandishing them. She reminded me of Don Quixote. The boys stepped back, saying, *whoa, whoa.*

I picked myself up. Don Quixote snatched my hand. She was still waving a recorder with the other. She led me, and we slipped quickly away. A parasol with lilies on it approached, little by little, then moved farther away. Soon, the school's green gate appeared. Once we'd passed through the gate, five corner stores welcomed us. My right hand, wet with blood from my nose, was still held in b's. I saw Glasses in the second store. He was peering into the ice cream freezer, holding his workbook in one hand. *Glasses!* I yelled. Glasses looked at me, surprised. I waved. He vanished into the distance immediately.

Soon thereafter we were passing Seoul Supermarket. Then we passed the Hahaha Karaoke Lounge and a convenience store, then Seoul Tours, Seoul Kitchen, Seoul Dental Clinic, and Seoul Eyewear, then every other *Seoul*, still running. I ran with my nose stained red. b ran with one hand gripping two recorders. I was gasping for air. My tongue lolled. The blood on my hand had dried, become powder, and fallen on the ground. The sky shook. A flock of seagulls flew around and around above my head. Salty sand clung to my cheeks. Flat, washed-out houses appeared. The road, and then the sky, widened. And then, here and there, the road started to vanish. There was sand scattered over the disappearing road. The road finally vanished altogether, and we jumped down onto the sand. When I lifted my head, I saw sky, the pale sun, and the breakwater. I saw the waves and the clouds spread low over them. I saw the sea.

13

At first, the water was cold. Second: the water was still cold. Third: the water was still cold. I rammed my head under and stretched out my legs. Fourth: the water was lukewarm. I stretched out my arms. Fifth: at last, the water began to feel warmer. I floated on top of the water, then sank. I opened my eyes and spread my arms wider. I could see shimmering boulders. They were drifting away. I pulled with my outstretched hands. Immediately, the boulders filled my vision. I covered my face with both hands. I could feel waves lightly pressing my back. I waited. I waited a little more.

Now.

Light poured down on me as I stretched my body. I watched the sky, which was the color of a well-ripened orange. b held my hand. She was as wet as a fish. I laughed. *Shh, the waves are coming.* I looked in the direction she pointed. A large mass of water and foam was surging toward us. Glaring at the waves, b took deep breaths. I raised my hand from the water. The blood had washed away without a trace. My nose was still a little swollen and hot. b continued to stare at the waves. In the sky, birds were drawing their lopsided circle; b and I swayed silently, only our heads above the water. *Now,* b said. I inhaled deeply. *One. Two.* b tightened her grip on my hand. We slid back below the water.

14

Three.

15

Those who no longer play in the water are called adults. Adults work in the city. They are the ones who don't see the sky, who no longer think about clouds, stars, seagulls, or the ocean.

Every weekend, adults seek out the shore with their children, carrying blankets and food. Their faces look as if they're bored out of their minds. Female adults wear enormous straw hats and rub sunscreen on their arms and faces every hour. Male adults stretch their legs and read the newspaper. And then they repeat over and over: *Don't wander too far off. Don't swim too far out. You're going to get cold. You're going to get hot. Stop crying. Stop being so loud. Sit still!* The adults, bored out of their minds, gather together with beers in their hands, smoke cigarettes, and grumble as they brush sand from their clothes. At night, the adults light a fire and barbecue. Sometimes a drunk man runs around howling like a wolf and jumps into the ocean. But he quickly gets back out. He looks bored out of his mind. No matter what they do, they look bored out of their minds. A face as stiff as a boulder, stiff with boredom—that's the face of an adult. Adults don't think about the ocean even when they watch it. Their minds are full of other things. It's very depressing to think that someday I, too, will be an adult.

Every Tuesday, b and I went to Alone. Alone was a café downtown. Adults thought the name was ridiculous and strange, but b and I thought it was cool. Too cool for such a boring neighborhood. Not surprisingly, the owner of Alone was from Seoul. He always wore nice sunglasses and sat under the sunshade in front of the café, reading some book with a cool name: *The Tragedy of Modern Civilization*; *The Fall of the Wall Street Empire*; stuff like that. Songs that seemed right for a coastal city flowed from the speakers. b wanted to work there, but Alone's owner told her that she was too young, and he would let her in two years. "When you're an upperclassman," he said. So b was waiting to become a junior. When I said, "I don't ever want to be an upperclassman," b said, "I'll give you free coffee. You can sit under the sunshade and do your homework." "Cool, I'd like that," I replied. Then b smiled, and I thought it was a relief that there would be at least one good thing in the future.

The reason we went to Alone every Tuesday was because drinks were half price on Tuesday afternoons. There were never any other customers on Tuesday afternoons. Sometimes, the owner gave us orange juice for free. But b didn't like orange juice. b said she would rather die than drink anything but coffee. At first, the owner said he wouldn't sell us coffee. "You're too young." "What does that have to do with coffee?" asked b, and then Alone's owner looked like he didn't know what to do. After five minutes, he said, "Fine, you win," and poured us each a half cup of coffee. Every time he'd say, "But this really is the last time, you're too young to be drinking coffee; you can have coffee when you're older."

When there weren't any other customers, it felt wonderful to lie on the worn-out green couch that smelled like coffee and cigarettes and listen to songs that seemed right for a coastal city. There were plenty of books on the bookshelves, and the owner would stand back with a serious look on his face while he picked out a book. When he did that, he looked pretty handsome and maybe even rich, maybe like a genius. "That guy, he's just running the café for fun," I once overheard my mom telling my dad. It was night, and I was lying on the couch in the living room. "In fact, I heard he was some kind of teacher in Seoul," she continued.

My dad replied, "No, I'm pretty sure I heard he was a car salesman. I think he's a distant relative of the family that runs Seoul Tours."

"No, they say he doesn't know anyone here."

"There's that one guy."

"Which guy?"

"That guy…remember?"

"Oh yeah, that guy… Anyway, the owner of the café is strange."

"He does seem pretty well off."

"Really?"

"Yeah, but you know…" And that's when I fell asleep. I was curious, but sleep won. Like always.

The owner of Alone truly was strange. As strange as the name of his café, and sometimes his oddity brought him attention. One day, a man who said he was a journalist from Seoul came to see Alone, carrying a huge camera and a small, thin computer. The man, who supposedly worked for a travel magazine, interviewed the owner of Alone and took a lot of photos of the café. And then, sometime later, a whole bunch of people came all at once, having searched out our city. They took photos at the beach and ate at the mall, then drank coffee at Alone and then they left. Or they drank coffee at Alone, ate at Seoul Kitchen, then hung out on the breakwater before spending the night at Seoul Motel. People closely examined the books on the bookshelves at Alone, swapped their own books for them, and took the new books home. They took tours around the city and said, "I really hate Seoul, I really want to live in a place like this." Then they asked about the prices of apartments downtown. Before leaving, they swore that they would come live here once they'd earned enough money, though no one had asked them about it. Of course, none of them came back. The owner of Alone hated those people. Fortunately, over time fewer and fewer people came, and in a few months they had stopped completely.

But no matter what, regardless of whether it was busy or not, late each night one person always came to Alone carrying a black plastic bag full of books. He'd stack the new books on the shelves, put the same number back in his bag, and then leave. His name was Book.

17

On my birthday I invited b and Glasses over to my house. I wasn't that close with Glasses, but he was the only boy in my class who didn't hit me or swear at me, so I also thought it would be nice to be better friends with him. My mom made japchae, bulgogi, and gimbab for us, but it was too much for just the three of us, so Mom decided she and Grandma would eat with us. None of us knew how to respond when Grandma said she refused to eat anything but candy.

"I'll give you some when you've finished eating your dinner," said b.

"I'll be too full to eat it then," said Grandma.

Glasses was wearing a very nice shirt, and in his hand was my present, rather than a workbook. He kept looking around awkwardly.

"I didn't have any money to buy anything," said b.

"It's okay," I said.

"Here, take this at least."

From her pocket, b took a piece of white paper that had been folded several times. It was a drawing of a horse. The horse was all the colors of the rainbow.

"Cool!" shouted Glasses. "You drew this?"

"Yeah…"

"This is so good!" Glasses' face showed his enthusiasm. b turned red.

"Really?"

"Totally!" I yelled.

"You're very good at drawing, b," my mom said. b's face grew redder. I examined the drawing carefully. The horse had a black mane tied back in two braids.

"So," explained b, "I thought you'd look nice if you wore your hair like this."

"This is me?" I asked.

"Yeah…" b said shyly.

"Thank you." I hugged her. "Thank you, thank you, thank you."

Glasses stood in the corner watching us, not knowing what to do. When I let go of b, Glasses handed me his present: "Open it."

"Okay," I said, and quickly unwrapped the paper. It was a fish-shaped cup. "Oh my!" my mom exclaimed, "A cup shaped like a fish!"

"I know!" said b.

"It…" stuttered Glasses, "it's from Seoul."

"It's so pretty!" I said. And then I almost hugged Glasses, but I glanced at b and it didn't seem wise to hug him, so I took a step back. "Thanks," I said again. Glasses smiled shyly.

This is awkward, I thought.

We started to eat our japchae, bulgogi, and gimbab. All of it was very good, and by the time we were finishing eating, the awkwardness had passed. Glasses talked about Seoul, and the rest of us just listened. I was toying with my fish cup, and b said she wanted one too. "I'll give you one on your birthday," said Glasses. "When is it?"

"It's already passed," said b. Her mood seemed to darken. "But it'll come again next year, though, right?" She finally said. Glasses nodded and b's face brightened.

After eating, we decided to go see a movie and set out from my house. On the bus to the movie theater, Glasses said, "I wish I was that good at drawing…"

"It's okay, you're smart instead," said b.

"But you got a hundred on your Korean test last time!"

"You remember that?" b said, surprised.

"Yeah, I graded yours," said Glasses proudly. "Of course, the teacher was with me…and I am the class president…" Glasses studied us nervously. "It's okay for me to grade tests if I'm the class president. Right?"

"Yeah, sure," said b, quickly averting her eyes to stare out the window. She began humming an unfamiliar song. Glasses bowed his head and rubbed his hands on his knees. *This is awkward*, I thought again.

The movie we saw was an animation about a fish. b had really wanted to see it, and it was fun. At every important scene, b muttered, "Whoa, whoa, whoa." And when the movie ended, she clapped, yelling, "Yay!"

I shouted too.

"Yeah…" Glasses said, glancing at us. We all smiled.

We were giddy as we went to Alone. It was Glasses' first time at the café, so he seemed a little nervous. No, actually, Glasses always seemed nervous, except when he was solving problems in his workbook.

As always, there weren't any customers at Alone when we arrived. Since it was a special occasion, the owner made lattes for all of us. The coffees were very weak, but there was enough caffeine to make our eyes sparkle. We got excited, and then very quickly surpassed mere excitement. Glasses took his glasses off. b started singing, her mouth open wide. We shook our clenched fists, not knowing what to do with them. A Cuban song was coming through the speakers. We sh-sh-shook our heads. The owner watched us and laughed. Gradually, the sun started setting. But in our hearts, it was still a bright and sunny day.

Suddenly, I shouted, "Why do the boys hate me?"

Glasses abruptly stopped dancing. So did b.

"What?"

"Why do the boys hate me? Why do they swear at me and hit me?" I was talking in a very loud voice. "What about you? Do you hate me too?" I asked Glasses.

Glasses groped around on the table for his glasses. "I…" He slowly put on his glasses. His eyes weren't shining anymore.

"I…" Glasses looked from me to b, back and forth. "I…" And then he said in a very small voice, "I don't hate you."

"Really?"

"Yeah, I don't hate anyone," Glasses said more confidently.

"Why not?" b asked.

"Well…because…" Glasses might've been on the verge of crying. But he held it in and replied, "Because it's bad to hate people."

"Says who?" asked b.

"It was in one of our textbooks."

"Well, I don't read textbooks, so I wouldn't know," said b.

"Me neither," I said.

"Well, that's what it says," said Glasses.

"Really?" I asked.

Glasses nodded.

"I see," b said, nodding.

"Okay," I said, also nodding.

"Yeah," Glasses nodded back.

18

It was a relief to spend my birthday with people who didn't hate me.

19

I know they're lying, though. But I'll pretend to believe it, since it's a nice thing to hear.

20

Cool.

21

It was during our writing class. The topic was friends, and I wrote about b. *I like b. I like b, who lives in a place that doesn't have a name. b, who is poor.* When it was my turn, I stood up and read what I'd written. *I like b, who is poor. I like b, even though she doesn't have anything, except a sick sister.* I had read that far when b got up from her seat, crossed the classroom, opened the door, and left. The kids started whispering among themselves. Interestingly, their expressions looked like the expressions of the boys when they hit me. The teacher's face was red. The teacher and her red face walked toward me. The classroom went as quiet as the inside of a rocket. She slapped me across the face. Then she took the piece of paper I'd been holding and ripped it into pieces. I couldn't cry because I didn't understand why I should. No one told me why. The blank faces gazing at me were like sheets of white paper. My face, which wasn't crying, looked like it usually did. Glasses scowled and pushed up his glasses. Everything was the same; they were all silently cursing me. I got angry: *Why are they acting like I did something wrong? I was just being honest.* The teacher went back to the front of the classroom. I stood up from my chair. "Sit down," the teacher said. I didn't sit down. "I told you to sit down!" The teacher shouted. I walked toward the door. "Where do you think you're going?" I opened the door. "Don't you dare leave!" I left. It's so easy, doing what you're not supposed to do. Things like that turn out to be so easy to do. I did it, and hoped something would change at least a little bit, but everything was still the same.

22

After that, b and I stopped hanging out together. I started going to Alone and to the beach alone. b ate lunch by herself then ran around the yard during recess. While b was running, the boys beat me. b didn't help me anymore when they hit me. I had to bear with it until it was over, then console myself. One day, b started eating lunch with the boys who beat me up. I ate lunch by myself, glaring at her as she ate with the boys who beat me up. b pretended like she didn't see me, tucking a lock of her hair behind her ear. All the kids avoided me even more than they had before.

The only one who didn't avoid me, although he didn't come over to me either, was Glasses. So, I just revolved around Glasses, around and around.

What a hard spring, I thought.

Glasses always ate his lunch with the vice president of our class. Next to the vice president sat Sky. Last year, Sky had it tough like I did now. But Sky was fine now, because of me. *I might be doing some good.* That's what I thought as I blotted the gash on my arm. But Sky never approached me; never talked to me; didn't even make eye contact with me. While Glasses and the vice president discussed our class's average math scores, I sat next to Glasses, silently nodding like a ghost. I watched Glasses. The vice president watched Glasses, too. Glasses looked at the vice president. Sky watched the vice president, too. I was a ghost. But I was grateful. Glasses never said anything like: *I'm sorry, but we don't have room for you to sit down.*

Suddenly, the door would open, and Sky would tremble. The boys that beat me up came in. Like always, they were wearing baseball caps. Names like "Tokyo," "Washington," "London," or "Shanghai" were embroidered on their caps. They all wore the same shirt as well, which had "Baseball" written across the chest. The boy who wore a Shanghai cap pushed past me, bumping into my shoulder. I fell to the ground with a spoon in one hand. Another boy took my plate and emptied it onto my head. Pieces of sautéed sausage and veggies slid down my cheeks. I curled up into a tight ball. *What a terrible spring,* I thought.

23

Some days, I go to school. Some days, I don't.

24

Walking home, my nose is as swollen as it was yesterday. My hand has as many wounds as yesterday. My blouse is as dirty as it was yesterday. My backpack has as many footprints on it as yesterday. My socks are as dirty as yesterday. And I'm as angry as I was yesterday. Yes, I'm angry. Too angry, terribly, really, really, *really*, but—

I don't know why.

I blink. Tears fall.

I don't wipe them. I just let them fall.

I see Dumpling, the tteokbokki place, in the distance. I had gone there often with b. She never had any money, so I bought her food for her. That's why I liked that b was poor. Because she was poor and because I liked b, I would have bought her tteokbokki every day. If b had been rich, she never would have drawn me something incredible like that rainbow horse for my birthday. Of course, I like Glasses' fish cup, but it was made in a factory in China, while b made the rainbow horse herself. Of course I like the rainbow horse better—I feel a little bad for Glasses, but I can't help it. Also, a nameless neighborhood is way cooler than an apartment building with a name. Since b's neighborhood doesn't have a name, I can make up one for it. I can call b's neighborhood *b*. "Where do you live?"

"Oh, I live in ShinDongAh Apartments Three." What a boring conversation. That's where Glasses lives, because ShinDongAh Apartments Three is bigger and newer and so much more expensive than One or Two. But it isn't fun to have people know how big my house is or how much the wallpaper cost. It's no fun to have no mystery. It's no fun to be no fun.

The ShinDongAh Apartments appear in the distance, which means that I'll get to Alone soon. What I really don't understand is why b is angry at me. That's that. Those ShinDongAh Apartments are *really* U-G-L-Y.

I pass by the ShinDongAh Apartments, then Alone. I pass by Hahaha Karaoke Lounge and the convenience store. All the while, I'm angry. Even that's the same as yesterday. I'm not angry because my scraped knee hurts. *Why am I angry? I don't even know.* Even that's the same as yesterday. Like yesterday, I go to the sea. My wounded hand, and b not being with me, is the same as yesterday. Everything is the same. And little by little, I feel…

Scared.

Yes, very scared. And that's the same as yesterday as well—feeling scared with my hair smelling like what I ate for lunch. How long will this continue? How long will I live this terribly identical day?

Maybe forever.

I stop walking and look up. As expected, nothing's different than yesterday. I look behind me. Still, nothing different.

It's the same.

Yes.

red, trickling letters said COMPLETE OPPOSITION. We didn't know what those words meant. "Do they mean they're so done that they're forced to oppose?"b had asked. I laughed. I laughed sweetly and innocently, the way a middle school student would laugh. Up on the chimney, people with chains around their bodies hugged each other tightly. Whenever they moved, you could hear the chains clanking. A helicopter circled like a seagull. Suddenly, there was a very strong gust of wind, and one of the people lost her footing. She hung, swaying, with the metal chain around her ankle. "Help!" people shouted. Immediately, a response flowed from the loudspeakers: "First, lift the strike." Eyes sparkling, we held our breaths. Men in black shirts carrying black clubs approached the strikers. Behind the men, people held up picket signs. And beyond them was the police. They covered the factory's entrance like the jet-black sea at night. The door was shut tight. Suddenly, the people with the picket signs let out a collective yell and started to climb the wall. The seagulls lifted off. The police swarmed in a jet-black wave. "You are creating a dangerous situation. Back up now," the speakers announced. "This demonstration is engaging in illegal activity." In the distance, we could see a large bus slowly crawling up the hill. On the wall, the picketers and police were entangled, fighting. A sharp scream slit the air. There was the sound of something hitting the ground. We looked back to the chimney—the person who had been dangling by her ankle was gone. A loose metal chain swayed in the air. The people still hanging onto the chimney wailed. The bus had crawled up the hill and was now stopped in front of an to take the road to the right. The road narrowed, and then even smaller paths split to either side. I changed directions randomly. Here and there, I saw worn-down houses. Eventually, there were so many houses they were lined up along a road. I remembered having seen those houses before. It was in a movie—a scene in which a woman in a kimono walks down a narrow road lined with two-story houses. In the movie, the road was very pretty. But this road, which looked exactly like the road in the movie, wasn't pretty at all. It was so narrow that it felt like my shoulders might touch the houses. The road barely continued, almost falling apart, almost collapsing. It felt like I should fall apart or collapse as well. At some point the wind had stopped blowing, but I couldn't see the sun. All the small windows were either broken or covered with sheets. The sheets looked dirty, in need of washing. The people who appeared from time to time were heaving along with crooked postures. They silently watched me with ill faces. They looked so sickly that I suddenly felt so healthy and good. The clothes they were wearing were so worn and dirty that suddenly my clothes felt clean. When I looked up again, kids were looking down at me through the windows. It was okay, though, because it didn't seem like they wanted to beat me up. I was relieved, but my pace still quickened. I was a little embarrassed—I don't know why, but I was. Another road appeared on the right, and I took it. But that place was the same, too. I changed directions again and again, but I was always in the same place. No, it was getting worse and worse. The sky was dark, like a thick blanket had been spread over me. The road smelled like a grandma who was dying. People were gasping for breath and lying on the ground. I turned and looked behind me. The houses were all the same. They were all the same decrepit two-story house. That was it. I started to sweat. I was so scared and so embarrassed. But, by what? I thought I was going to puke from the smell that dug into my nose and mouth. I wanted to see the sky. But I couldn't. Everything was too black. It was too black.

28

It would've been better to just go to the sea—it would've been nice to watch the gulls. I should've just gone to the supermarket for some ice cream. It would've been nice to sit on the beach. I should've gone to the mall and taken the escalator. I should've watched a movie. I should've gone to Alone. No. I should've just gone home. I should've taken a road I recognized. Yes. I should've just…just taken a road I knew.

29

It was like being in a really bad dream that would never end. The sky looked like it would stay night forever. It felt like those rows of houses would continue to the edge of the world. The road would never end. At last, I realized—this was the End. I recalled the stories Grandma had told me. I just gave up and closed my eyes. Tears gathered behind my closed lids. I thought of my mom, of Grandma, my dad,

Glasses… I started to silently cry. For a long time, I stood and cried, until I heard a small sound. I opened my eyes and saw something coming toward me. It was a huge fish. The fish had purple scales covering its body, and whenever it moved its fins, rays of light spread like waves. *It's so pretty,* I thought. The fish came closer and closer, and the light grew brighter. It stopped, just in front of my chest. The fish's eyes shined like it was also crying. I reached out and touched its fin. It was as cold as ice. The fish blinked, once, and a tear fell. Then it started moving again. I kept still as the fish slowly passed through my body. I closed my eyes.

Only for a second.

I opened them.

The fish was gone.

I could feel it getting colder. The darkness and the unpleasant, warm air were fading away. I started walking again. Over time the houses receded, dead trees and pieces of trash taking their place. My fear was gone. I was still in the End. But it was okay, now. *Yes, it's okay*, I thought. And at the end of the road I found some stairs.

It was a very old stone stairway. A collapsed stone wall with grass growing in the cracks lay next to it. The stairs went so far up that I couldn't see where they ended. I started to climb, still not knowing where I was or where the stairway led. But it didn't matter. I went faster. After a while I looked up and saw the factory on my right. The factory, blanketed with white smoke. To my left were the lower sections of stairs I had already climbed, and trash, and the End. It was now far enough away to see it all together in a single glance.

After climbing for quite some time, huge trees began to appear, in ones and twos, alongside the stairs. The trees thickened, turning into a forest. The stairs continued on. I was hungry. My legs hurt and I was worried about the long walk back home. *If my mom asks, "Where did you go?" I'll have to lie and say I was playing with b,* I thought. But first I would have to get back home. *From now on, I'm going to only take paths I know. If I ever find my way home at all, that is.* I cried a little more.

As the wind blew, the leaves swayed and danced in the light. The wind carried the scents of fresh trees and the ocean. The ocean? I suddenly knew where I was—I was climbing the North Hill. I cheered softly, and then the stairway ended.

There was a small field, surrounded by large trees. I crossed the field and entered the forest. Then the forest disappeared. Suddenly, all the trees were hidden behind me. Just like magic. No, like a magic curse being broken. And the sky came back. I almost cried again. I was so glad to see the sky. *Sky, it's been too long.* I greeted the sky and it greeted me, too, with even brighter sunlight. I was so happy I curled like a strawberry vine. Under the sky a green grassy field glistened in the sunlight. The field stretched to a cliff, and the cliff touched the clouds. And beyond all of it was the sea.

I started to run.

Good to see you, sea. It's been a long time.
Good to see you too, seagull. It's been a long time.
Good to see you too, clouds.
Good to see you. It's so, so good to see all of you.

Good to…

And then I saw a square box in a corner of the field. It sat under a very large tree. It was a small house. I knew that because a door opened and a person came out. He was wearing a black shirt and held a trash bag in one hand.

My eyes went wide and I took a step back.

He also took a step back.

It was Book.

30

I walked toward him.

He took another step back.

"You're Book…right?"

Book didn't answer. He looked a little bewildered and up close he seemed a lot younger than I had thought he was. If you took away his beard, he'd kind of look like a college student.

"You're Book, right?" I asked again.

"Yeah," Book replied. Then he stuck his hands in his pockets and looked down his nose at me with an arrogant expression. The black plastic bag in his left hand swung back and forth. "How'd you find this place?"

"Well…that's…"

Book scratched his neck and yawned.

"Damn, I was going to take a nap."

"Sorry."

"Obviously, you're lost."

I nodded.

"I don't get it. Why do people who're lost always end up here, of all places? There's a kid or two every year. Usually they're crying and have dirt all over their faces. Not you, though. That's good at least." As he was talking, Book nodded, looking like he really was impressed.

"I've seen you before," I said.

"I've seen you, too."

"At Alone?"

"No, at the breakwater."

"You go to the breakwater, too?"

"Sure, why not?" he asked.

I stood perfectly still.

"You keep getting beaten up, right? By those boys with baseball caps. Right?" he said.

I continued standing, not saying anything.

"You don't wanna talk about it? Are you ashamed? Don't bother with that—human beings are such shameful creatures by nature."

"Why didn't you help me?"

"What?"

"You said you saw me. So why didn't you help?"

"Well…that's…" Book was at a loss for words.

"If you saw that, you should've helped me."

Book couldn't say anything.

"Say something. Huh?"

Book dropped his head.

"Sorry. I didn't think. Next time I promise I'll help."

"Of course you should help."

"Don't you need to go back home?"

"I will. But down there, is that the End?"

"What's the End?"

"The End. You know, the End."

"What's that?"

"The End. Where the people who are ruined live."

"I don't know about that."

"Never mind, then."

"The End—killer name, though."

Book bowed his head again and chuckled, looking like the foolish villain in a comic book. But once he stopped laughing, he went back to looking like a college student.

"What time is it?"

"I dunno. Wait here a minute, I'll check," Book said, going back into the house. I walked toward the house as well. "Four thirty!" he yelled, coming back outside. "The sun will set soon. You need to hurry back home."

"I don't want to."

"Why not?"

"I'm hungry."

"What's that supposed to mean?"

"It means I'm hungry."

"Are you asking me for food?"

"Yes."

Book was startled.

"Why are you so surprised?" I asked.

"You're a bold kid," he said, chuckling again. "I have food, but…"

"But what?"

"Whatever. Nothing."

Book crossed his arms.

"So are we going to eat or not?" I demanded.

Book glared at me. I made a pitiful face.

"Damn it," Book sighed.

Book's house looked like a house built from books. All sorts of them were piled everywhere, from floor to ceiling. There were novels, comics, cookbooks, history books, children's books, science books, Bibles, music books, art books, even a middle school textbook, the one I'd used at school a couple of years ago.

"Just take a seat wherever." Book moved some books onto the floor to make space for me. He poured water into a kettle and put it on the stove. I stared at him absentmindedly and his eyes met mine as he turned back from the stove.

"What?" he asked.

"Huh?"

"Why are you looking at me like that?"

"I don't know what you're talking about… Are these all your books?"

"Yeah… Is a cup of ramyeon okay?"

"Yeah, I like ramyeon."

Book laughed, "Yeah, kids always like ramyeon."

I picked up a comic book from a corner.

"Hey…" I began.

"Huh?"

"Why do you live out here?"

"It's a free country."

"That's it?"

Book looked at me. His eyes, staring straight at me, were deep and sharp.

"No, I mean, like, is that the only reason?"

"I don't like the city," Book said, shaking his head. "No…I don't like people."

"Why not?"

"Do you like the city?"

"I don't know. I've never really thought about it."

"By the way, it's a secret that you saw me here today, that I live here."

"Why?"

"If the city finds out, they might evict me and demolish the house."

"What's evict mean?"

"It means they'll kick me out of here."

"But everyone knows you live out here."

"No, they think I live down there, not up here."

"You mean down in the End?"

Book knit his brow and put a bowl of kimchi in front of me.

I grabbed a piece and put it in my mouth.

"The kimchi's good."

"It's from the store."

"Ah."

"How are you planning on getting home? The sun's basically down already."

Book put the instant ramyeon in front of me and went outside. I opened the lid. The delicious smell clung to my nose. My stomach was squalling for food. But the moment I put the noodles in my mouth I froze. Through the half-open door, a picture like from a dream was unfolding. I walked outside with my cup of ramyeon in one hand. The golden-orange sky looked like a sea that had become black tea. "So pretty," I said aloud. Then, for some strange reason, I felt sad. I closed my eyes and counted to ten before opening them again. The sea of black tea was still spread out before me. I looked over my shoulder. Book's house was also tinted the color of black tea. His hair was the color of black tea. And the cigarette he held, too. Black tea-colored smoke silently blended with the black tea-colored sky.

I don't want to go home, I thought.

And slowly I started to eat my ramyeon.

My Sister

Whenever I look around, I'm alone.

Everyone avoids me.

It seems so easy to be with people,

but it's so hard for me.

1

I have a younger sister.
    That's it.

2

I don't like my sister. I could fill a whole book about that.
    But I don't want to.

3

I don't have any friends. Well, I did have one friend. Her
name was Rang. Rang liked me and I liked her. We hung
out every day; had a lot of fun. If I held Rang's hand, she
held mine. When Rang linked her arm in mine, my chest
swelled with pride. If I told her I wanted ice cream, she'd
buy some for me. We'd share the ice cream, taking turns

licking it. Licking ice cream, we'd walk to the shopping mall, ride the escalator until it got boring—looking at all the mannequins on display, looking at the pretty people— then we'd take the elevator to the movie theater. The elevator was quiet and incredibly fast. The moment its doors opened, the sweet smell of popcorn would fill my nose. I liked that a lot, and so did Rang.

On the way home, we'd buy tteokbokki at Dumpling. Rang would buy it for me.

On my last birthday, she got me a scarf, because my birthday is in the winter. On Rang's birthday, I drew her a rainbow horse, because I'm poor.

When the baseball boys beat up Rang, I charged them with a recorder in each hand.

That was then.

I don't do that anymore, because we're no longer friends. Because I'm poor and Rang's not poor. And not-poor Rang just pisses me off. I was once not-poor, too. That was a very long time ago, but I still remember what it used to be like. Especially when I'm with Rang; when I watch Rang, I remember when I wasn't poor. I used to live in the city, too—our lives could've ended up being very similar, Rang's and mine. But not anymore. We're different. We're very different now. I get so angry thinking about this stuff. No, I want to cry. I want to scream and I want to swear. But it doesn't bother Rang. Why would it? She doesn't need to cry or scream or swear. But I'm not like her. It bothers me a lot, which is why I don't hang out with Rang anymore, why we aren't friends anymore. I don't run to protect her with the recorder in my hand anymore. I don't do that.

The baseball boys bully Rang because they're bored. It's not about who Rang is, or that kid Sky who got bullied before her. It doesn't matter as long as they're beating someone up. They're bored because they have to throw a baseball a hundred times and hit the ball a hundred times and run around the baseball diamond a hundred times every day. Every single day, or else the coach beats them. On the days when the coach punishes them, they hit Rang even harder. She never cries, no matter how hard they hit her, which makes the baseball boys really mad, so they beat her more and more violently. But still, Rang doesn't cry. Even if I stand with the baseball boys and watch her getting beaten up, Rang doesn't cry. She calmly tries to crawl away. They laugh and kick her in the butt. With one hand over her butt, Rang continues to crawl, calmly.

I know that Rang never cries and never will.

I try to look as composed and peaceful.

But it's really hard.

4

When Rang and I were friends, we always went to the beach together. Rang took her shoes off and walked in the sand. So did I. Rang dove into the ocean. So did I. Rang got out of the water. So did I. We went back in together.

We got wet.

The two of us, we both got exactly equally wet.

Once, as Rang climbed into the waves, I held back. Wet Rang rolled in the sand, which clung to her body like breadcrumbs. We laughed. I put my hands in my pockets and laughed. Rang went in and out of the water. There were more and more grains of sand clinging to her body. She shook her head. Wet sand fell on top of dry sand. Rang laughed and so did I. She laughed louder and I laughed louder. Then, abruptly, I stopped.

The face of my sister had popped into my head.

I always stop laughing when I think about her, and the problem is that I always remember her when I'm laughing. That's why I don't like to laugh. I'm usually thinking about her, regardless of whether I'm laughing or not. She clings to my head, like the sand on Rang's body. One big, heavy grain of sand, like an iron ball. That's why I'm always tired. Another iron ball clings to my left leg. There's one around my neck, and one on each finger. They hang from my pockets, my backpack, and from my underwear, too. The iron balls drag me into the ground, under the ground, deeper and deeper. It's really dark down there. I can't see anything. It's so scary. But I can't scream for help, because I don't want anyone to see me. I don't want anyone to see the iron balls that hang from my pockets, from my lips, dangling like apples from a tree. I'd rather die.

I scowl to keep the tears in.

And bite my lips.

Rang laughs. Her laughter grows louder and louder. More iron balls on my body, growing fatter and heavier.

I frown even harder. I can't seem to smooth it out. And then Rang looks over and sees my face. My scrunched up, scowling face. The laughter dies.

5

Rang stops laughing.
I just ruined everything, I think.

6

I run. Or it's more like I escape. My hands, fingers spread, cover my face as I run. Rang calls my name, but I don't respond. Rang runs after me, calling my name. My face is hot. It grows hotter and hotter. I'm so embarrassed. I want to disappear.

7

They say the place where I live now used to be a swamp. Then, one hot summer, somebody poured tons of sand into the swamp, flattened it out, then built houses on top of it. I don't know if that's a true story. It might just be something they say.

If you open my window, you'll see a factory. The chimney of a factory. It's so big that there are no words to describe how big it is. Puffs of white smoke always curl out of the big chimney. The smoke smells like soy sauce, but it's supposedly very bad for your health. My house always smells like soy sauce.

A lady lives next door. I don't like her. She's always bringing food over to our house. The lady works at a restaurant inside a shopping plaza in the city. Last year, my family went to eat there for my sister's birthday. The lady gave her a pair of pajamas, which she liked a lot. That night I secretly took the pajamas and threw them away. My sister cried when she found out.

Sometimes the lady brings grilled mackerel over to our house. I don't like that.

Sometimes the lady brings bulgogi over to our house. I don't like that.

This afternoon, the lady brought us kimchi. I wanted to punch her smiling face. After she left, I woke up my sister. "Hey, throw this away." She slowly rubbed her eyes, half asleep. I hit her in the head. "Are you awake yet?" She didn't reply. She still looked half asleep. "I said, throw this away. Can't you hear me? Are you deaf? Or are you so sick you've lost your mind? Or maybe you can't talk anymore. Is that it?" I hit her in the head again. She started to cry. "Be quiet… I said, throw this away." I glared at her. She got up and started to put on her jacket, still crying. *What would the lady say if she saw me right now?* I thought. *She'd probably be upset. She might even cry too. I want to make her cry. I want to do something.* I turned on the television. Nothing good was on. I lay down on my stomach.

Sister

What?

Sister

Startled, I jumped to my feet.

Sister

It was the sound of the door rattling. No, the windows. No, the door. Both.

Sistersistersistersistersister

The floor shook. And the windows, the ceiling, the whole apartment.

"Ah!" I covered my ears and curled up on the floor.

Sistersistersistersistersistersistersistersistersistersister sistersistersistersistersistersistersistersistersistersister sistersistersistersistersistersistersistersistersistersister sistersistersistersistersistersistersistersistersistersister sistersistersistersistersistersistersistersistersistersister sistersistersistersistersistersistersistersistersistersister sistersistersistersistersistersistersistersistersistersister sistersistersistersistersistesistersistersistersistersister sistersistersistersistersistersistersistersistersistersister sistersistersistersistersistersistersistersistersistersister sistersistersistersistersistersistersistersistersistersister sistersistersistersistersistersistersistersistersistersister sistersistersistersistersistersistersistersistersistersister sistersistersistersistersistersistersistersistersistersister sistersistersistersistersistersistersistersistersistersister

"I'm sorry," I cried out. "Please. Please forgive me. I won't do it again."

But it was no use. The shaking grew worse.

Am I going to die?

No!

"I'm sorry!"

Suddenly, everything went still. I looked up to see my sister standing in front of me. I had been crouching, but I sat on the floor. She looked sick, like always. "I'm hungry," I said. She looked at me, her face sad. "Go make me some ramyeon." Without replying, she went into the kitchen and turned on the stove.

The ramyeon she makes is very good, because of how often I make her cook it.

While my sister cooked, I turned on the television. On came ads for cars, makeup, houses, and a special kimchi refrigerator. The ads ask me to please buy their nice, fancy products. I really do want to buy them, but I don't have any money. It's depressing to think about. My sister came into the room with the pot of ramyeon. Still angry, I realized we were out of kimchi. I can't eat ramyeon without kimchi. I wondered if I should make her go out and buy some. But we didn't have any money. Briefly, I toyed with the idea of making her steal kimchi from the supermarket. I shook my head. "I'm not hungry anymore," I said. "You eat it."

My sister does whatever I tell her to do. I hit her if she doesn't. Whenever she's holding back tears, frightened, it reminds me of Rang getting beaten by the baseball boys. *That* reminds me of Washington Hat, the way he sometimes smiles as he kicks her. I wonder if it makes more sense for me to hang out with him instead of Rang. I watch my sister eat ramyeon and think about Washington Hat and Rang. Tears roll down her cheeks. She eats the ramyeon in silence.

8

On TV was a show about a lizard. The lizard's name was Lucky. He lived in a big glass box in the spacious living room of an apartment in Seoul. But ten days ago, Lucky had decided to stop eating. So, Lucky's owner, a nine-year-old boy, took him to the veterinarian. The vet told him that Lucky had a disease that filled his stomach with rocks. That's why Lucky couldn't eat. The boy started to cry. It was really annoying to watch him cry. It was really annoying when he said, "Please don't die."

The doctor replied, "We'll try our best," and they began the surgery. The boy cried himself to sleep on his mom's lap. When he woke up, the surgery was over and the door to the operating room opened just as he got up from his seat. The doctor took off her mask. Apparently, the surgery had been a success. The boy and his mom rejoiced. In the next scene, Lucky was in a clean terrarium with white bandages wrapped around his body. The boy stroked his head. "You were so strong." I looked over at my sister. She looked happy, too. Her eyes were sparkling with joy as she watched the show.

"Don't worry," I said. "It'll die soon. And if it doesn't, I'll find it and kill it. There's no such thing as miracles." I smiled. "It's all a damn lie. We all die. And," I said, looking straight into her eyes, "you'll die first." The light in my sister's eyes had died. "Don't worry about it. Don't worry about anything at all."

9

I started to hang out with Washington Hat.

10

During recess, Washington Hat sat me on his lap. I didn't stop him. Washington Hat put both of his hands around my waist. I let him. Washington Hat touched my breasts. I didn't care. Rang was watching, but I pretended not to notice.

After school, Washington Hat brought me to an alley. The baseball boys were there, smoking cigarettes. I crossed my arms and watched them smoke. All of them were wearing hats. *I want a hat, too,* I thought. I couldn't afford one, but I wanted one. I pushed Washington Hat's arms away from around my waist.

"What?" he asked.

"I want a hat." Washington Hat looked at me seriously. "A *hat*, the thing on your head." I pointed to Washington Hat's hat.

"You really want one?"

"Yeah."

Washington Hat blew cigarette smoke from his mouth. "Okay, I'll buy you one." He threw his cigarette on the ground. "C'mon, let's go," Washington Hat shouted. The other baseball boys just nodded. "Let's go!" Washington Hat crossed his arms and narrowed his eyes. Everyone hurriedly exhaled smoke and threw their cigarettes to the ground.

Reeking of cigarettes, we arrived back at school. I tried to look bored, just like the others. But it was clear I wasn't one of them, since I didn't have a hat. I looked at Washington Hat, terribly jealous of the Washington hat sitting squarely on his head. "I thought we were going to go buy me a hat."

"I know, that's what I said."

"Then why are we at school?"

"Hey…here he comes!" shouted London Hat. I looked up. It was Glasses. Reading from a math workbook he held in one hand, he walked toward us. "Hey, Glasses!" Washington Hat yelled. Glasses looked up. When he saw Washington Hat, Glasses' face turned as white as milk. "Going home?" Washington Hat yelled. Glasses squirmed a little but didn't reply. "Come here for a second." Glasses hesitated. "I said, come here!"

"What…what do you want?"

"Come here and I'll tell you."

Glasses started slowly walking over, very slowly. And then he saw me.

"Hurry up!"

Now Washington Hat was walking toward Glasses, who immediately stopped in his tracks.

Washington Hat grinned.

"Got any money on you?"

"No, I don't."

Glasses looked at me. I quickly looked down.

"You don't?"

Glasses didn't reply. Washington Hat grabbed him by the neck. Glasses made a choking noise that sounded like *khek!* Washington Hat threw him backward. Glasses collapsed on the ground. The baseball boys jumped on him. "Wait," said Washington Hat. The boys immediately stood back, like obedient dogs. Washington Hat stooped down, grabbed Glasses' bag, unzipped it, and took out a wallet. There was a ten thousand won bill inside. Washington Hat tucked the bill in his pocket and grabbed Glasses again, forcing him to his feet.

"Why did you lie?" Washington Hat slapped Glasses across the cheek with the empty wallet. "I hate liars more than anything in the world," he said. "Right? You guys all know how much I hate liars, right?"

"Definitely, yeah," nodded the boys. Washington Hat turned back to Glasses, who was trembling all over. "I asked you a question."

Glasses couldn't reply. He just continued to tremble.

"Damn it!" Washington Hat said and kicked Glasses. A groan leaked out of Glasses. Washington Hat spit on Glasses' glasses.

Washington Hat looked at me: "Let's go hat shopping."

And then he smiled, which was kind of cute.

"Okay," I responded.

And then I crossed my arms and made a bored face. Washington Hat put an arm around my waist. It popped into my head that I wanted a pair of sunglasses more than a hat.

11

Washington Hat really did buy me a hat. It was yellow and had the word WASHINGTON across the front. We ate ramyeon with the change.

12

My sister takes her medicine five times a day. Five pills each time. A pink pill, a white pill, a red pill, another white pill, and then pink again. When it's time to take her medicine, I get her a cup of water. "Hey, drink this." She puts the pills in her mouth and swallows them in one gulp. But today the gulp was so loud and irritating. Her face was yellow and swollen, like a piece of bread with eyes attached to it. I got angry. I just happened to be wearing the Washington hat, which could be why I was even angrier than usual—Washington Hat had said it would do that. It was after he got drunk. I had gotten drunk, too. We were sitting on the couch in the house of one of Washington Hat's friends. "I'm so fucking angry." That was what he said. I was lying with my head on his stomach, or maybe in his lap.

"Fucking angry about what?" I asked.

"I don't know," Washington Hat said and started to jiggle his leg. My head jiggling up and down. "I'm just fucking angry."

"I get like that too, sometimes." I sat up.

"So fucking angry, goddamn," said Washington Hat.

"Me too!" But Washington Hat wasn't listening to me, which might have been a good thing. Otherwise he might have gotten even angrier and hit me. Washington Hat looked mad, but he didn't seem to have a focus. It scared me.

Looking at my sister, that's exactly how angry I was. *I'm so pissed*, I thought. *I'm going to crush this piece of bread until she's the size of a ball and stuff her into the trashcan.* She was crying. I looked around the room to see what else I could do. The paper bag holding her pills was on the floor. I grabbed it and ripped it in half. Pills scattered on the ground. My sister's eyes bulged as wide as baseballs. I ripped the paper bag in half again.

"Stop that!" she yelled. "Stop doing that!" As she yelled, she started picking up the pills that were spread across the floor. Her back was hunched, like the handle of a teacup. *Like a bug*, I thought. *Oh my god.* I fled from the room, screaming.

13

The road was gray. Actually, it was black and narrow, like a thin string. And I was sinking into it. The ashy string arched over me, curving like that teacup handle. *Oh my god.* I put my hands on top of my head. The Washington hat was there, tight. I couldn't take it off. It was like my sister was sitting on top of the hat hugging a huge iron ball tightly. That's why I was sinking. The ground was bottomless. I kept sinking deeper and deeper, all because of my sister.

It wasn't like this before. When she was healthy, my sister didn't weigh on my head like this. She even knew how to laugh, and wasn't like a piece of bread in any way. But, when had she ever not been sick? It seems like she's been sick since before I was born. So I've had a sick sister since before I was born. Thanks. Thanks to her, my life will always suck. I'll live miserably and die miserably. With all sorts of weird things dangling from my head. "Thanks a lot!" I yelled. "I'm so grateful that I could destroy everything!" I pressed down on my head—no, on the hat. It hurt. But I wanted to hurt even more.

Then I won't need to think about anything!

But the thoughts kept coming. Things like: My sister makes really good ramyeon. But she can't eat ramyeon. She throws up afterward, because she's sick.

I started walking again. Suddenly, in front of me was a set of stairs. It was long and tall, stretching so far into the distance that it almost touched the sky. As I looked at it, the iron was growing. The balls got bigger and there were more of them. *Grow more!* I shouted in my head. *Grow more! More! More!* I collapsed to the ground and started crying. Iron balls dangled from all over my body. After crying for a long time, I was getting up when something jingled in my pocket. I stuck my hand in and found some money. Two hundred and thirty won. *What should I do with this?* I thought. I might be able to make a phone call. But to whom? Should I call home? And then? Scream at my sister, tell her I'll kill her? Scream at her to just die? Scream at her and say I'll kill her if she's not dead by the time I get home? But our house doesn't even have a phone. We used to have one, but our mom got rid of it because of all the calls from creditors. When she got rid of our phone, she explained to us that we didn't need it. She said she didn't need a phone because she was at the factory all day. My sister didn't need a phone since she stayed home all day. I didn't need a phone since I was at school. Only our dad needed one, but he had a cellphone. Should I call my dad? But I can't do that, because I skipped school today. Instead of going to school, I ripped up my sister's bag of pills, yelled at her, made her cry. Then I skipped lunch and now I'm crying on the street. I can't call Rang because we aren't friends anymore. I can't call Washington Hat, because he keeps trying to touch my chest. I don't like it. When Washington Hat touches my chest, I feel like a dog—he strokes my chest as though he's stroking a dog, since that's the only way he can think of to touch a chest. Or sometimes he hits me, but I don't want to be hit, so I let him stroke me like a dog. It's better than getting hit. Honestly, it all feels wrong. But I don't want to think or feel. The iron balls grow whenever I do that. And when they grow, my head hurts, and then, and then…

What should I do with 230 won?

Suddenly, I felt bad about the 230 won—I couldn't seem to think of a meaningful way to use it. I should just eat it. I put the coins in my mouth but pretty quickly I gagged and my mouth fell open. Two hundred and thirty won, spit, and blood came out. Nothing else came up though, because I hadn't eaten anything. I lifted my head. The sun—small and flat as a dime—was in the sky. I began walking again. The road seemed endless—like the flight of stairs. It occurred to me that I might not be able to escape. Ever. Until I died. Even after I died. *I'll walk and then I'll die and die and die and die,* I muttered to myself as I passed an empty rice store. I passed a dog lying so still it seemed dead. I passed an old hardware store. I passed a burned down stationery store. Through the smashed window, I could see a dead clock and burned wallpaper and a smashed up robot. I felt like burned wallpaper, like a smashed up robot. No, it felt like I was beginning to *belong* here. It was frightening. I was no longer simply walking down the street, but was trapped between rows of dead houses. It wasn't a street, but a tiny crack. And the crack was about to close.

I stopped walking. All of a sudden, the crack was gone. As swiftly and easily as a single blink of the eye. I swallowed. The sound of the gulp echoed up the streets. Then it was completely silent, and in the distance, I could see smoke floating straight up from a chimney. Drying laundry swayed on a rooftop. A hat was on my head. I opened my mouth. Nothing came out. Only what sounded like ragged breathing.

14

Some people are born to be alone. That's what I said. We were at Alone. I was sitting on an old green couch. Rang stood in front of me. She was wearing a red school uniform and red high-top sneakers. A name tag that read *Rang Hong* was clipped to her chest. *You're born like that,* I continued. *And when you're born like that, you can't escape it.* I touched my head. Sure enough, the hat was there. *It sticks to you and won't come off, like this hat.* Rang looked at me, but she wasn't really looking at me. We were in two different times: I was at Alone on Wednesday; Rang was at Alone on Friday afternoon. *Whenever I look around, I'm alone,* I said. *Everybody avoids me. It seems so easy to be with people, but it's so hard for me.* Rang was with other people. They were all wearing red school uniforms. My sister, Mom, Dad, Glasses, the baseball boys, and Washington Hat. I kept talking. Everyone was looking in my direction, but they weren't looking at me. Only I could see them. *I was born this way. That's why I'm alone. Why I'm lonely.* My words were invisible and quickly crumbled. Suddenly, the people started to disappear, one by one. I didn't do anything. Rang was the last to disappear. Then I woke up. I woke up alone and friendless.

15

Before, only my dad went to the factory. No one else needed to work. We lived in the city then. I took piano lessons and my sister took taekwondo. Every weekend, we packed lunch and a mat and went to the beach. Dad would inflate the boats, and we'd row or just float in the water. When we were out deep, my sister would dive in. I'd wear heart-shaped sunglasses. Her too. She made sandcastles and I snuck around her to step on them, making her cry. Then I'd buy her ice cream. No, I stole ice cream from Highway Grocery. When I'd give her the stolen ice cream, she'd stop crying. After eating it, she'd lie on the mat and fall asleep. I'd put my mouth close to her ear and yell, making her cry again. Mom would get angry with me, and then I'd start crying. I'd cry until I fell asleep next to my sister. When I woke up again, the sun would be setting. The beach teeming with adults. They'd start a fire and cook meat over it. I'd rub my eyes and totter over to the grill. My mom would give me a nicely cooked piece of meat. I opened my mouth wide like a baby bird.

It all made me happy. I loved my sister. She wasn't sick yet.

Now that she's sick, I hate her.

Our family is different now. We don't go to the beach anymore. On the weekends, my mom and dad lie in their bedroom and watch television. They watch TV until they doze off. They sleep until they wake back up to watch more TV. They sleep more, then they wake up to smoke cigarettes and eat ramyeon. Dad drinks soju. Then he lies down on the floor. Night falls. I turn off the light. We lie down in our beds. We fall asleep. That's all. That's my family's weekend.

During the week, when my mom comes home from work, she asks my sister if she took her medicine on time, whether she feels better or worse, if she cried because of the pain, and what she did. She doesn't ask me anything. One day, she came home while my sister was making ramyeon for me. She got really angry, slapped me on the face, and asked me why I didn't just die already. I told her it wasn't me, but my sister who should die. My mom cried. So did my sister, but I didn't. I held my tears.

My mom definitely told me to die, which means she hopes that I die. My parents have never cared about me. That's why they don't give me any money. I'm sick of not having money. Really, really sick of it. Sick of asking Washington Hat to buy me ramyeon. Sick of stealing from stores and from people and wearing my Washington hat around all the time. But above all, I'm sick of my sister. I really do wish she would hurry up and die. After she dies, I'll be able to love her again. After she dies, I'll get to be terribly sad. I'll bring flowers to her grave and cry every day. But until she dies, I can't do anything. I can't do anything except make her life miserable.

How nice would it be if I had a billion won? With a billion won, we could take her to the hospital in Seoul. And I wouldn't have to hate her. I could do nothing but pray for her all day. With money, we could go to after-school tutoring again. I might get better grades than Glasses. Then maybe we could be friends. Maybe I'd go out with Glasses instead of Washington Hat. Maybe Glasses wouldn't touch my breasts the way Washington Hat does. Maybe he would touch them in a more polite and smarter way. But I don't have a billion won, so I can't do anything. If she were rich, my sister could go to medical school, study hard, and become an excellent doctor. But since she doesn't have money, even if she got accepted to medical school, she wouldn't have time to study because she'd be working to pay her tuition. I knew someone like that. His dad was friends with my dad. He was really smart, got straight As, and managed to get into a college in Seoul. But it was too expensive, so he gave it all up and came back here. He did nothing but drink for three months, then enlisted in the military. Since he got discharged, he's been working at my dad's factory. Apparently, he's saving up to study for the civil service exam. I'm scared I'll end up like him. Actually, I'm definitely going to end up like him. Dreams are expensive, which is why I can't have one. If I only had a billion won, I could have a really cool and expensive dream. But I don't have a billion won. I have exactly one thousand won, which I stole from my mom's purse. I don't know what to do with it. I really don't know… If I just had a billion won, my sister wouldn't die, Mom wouldn't have to work at the factory, and even I could become a doctor. But since I only have a thousand won, my sister will die, my mom will continue working at the factory, and I'll grow up to be trash.

16

Rang is almost always alone these days. When she's not, it's because she's getting beaten up. Or she doesn't show up to school at all. Sometimes she's with Glasses. The baseball kids call him a retard. *You… retard. Hey, retard, come over here. You fucking retard, where you going?* And occasionally they take his money and go to the convenience store. But they don't hit him that often, because the teachers like Glasses. Also, swearing and calling him retarded is enough to make Glasses plenty scared. But Rang isn't afraid of them, which is why she keeps getting beaten up. And because our teachers don't like Rang—when they see her getting beaten up, the female teachers tilt their parasols slightly to hide it from view. The male teachers cross their arms and look up at the sky while Rang gets beaten in the middle of the baseball field. The beatings seem more frequent these days. But I don't care about that. Standing next to Washington Hat, I watch her getting beaten. I watch Washington Hat punch her. Before, he would kick her a few times and that was it, simply killing time. Now, the blows are harder and there are more of them. Rang goes home covered in dirt and blood every day. Watching her stagger home with blood on her white blouse and her hair disheveled, I think Washington Hat might kill her soon. But I still don't do anything. Nothing. Maybe I want Rang to die. She keeps appearing in my dreams. I can't sleep.

17

Everyone is standing. I'm the only one sitting. With a pencil in one hand, I look down at my desk. I don't think about anything; I don't see anything; I don't expect anything. The hat is in my bag. I take it out and put it on. Rang's seat is still empty. I keep checking on her. It's stupid. I see a bunch of hats through the window. I know what's happening but wish I didn't. Maybe the hat caused everything. I take it off. I put it back on. There are seven minutes of recess left. I still have the pencil in my hand. I swap it for a pen, then begin to draw a picture on my desk. I can't draw. There's nothing I do well, which is why I don't have any friends. I had one friend. Her name was Rang, and when I hung out with her, everyone made fun of me. They kept their distance and quietly mocked me. Nobody mocks me now. Even though I'm not really friends with Washington Hat. Even though he strokes me like I'm a dog. I wonder what will happen if I stop hanging out with him. He's going to call for me soon. Rang, Washington Hat, and me—the three of us seem to be forming a weird triangle. And I think I caused everything. But I had no intention of getting Rang beaten up. I just…just… This is what I think: *It's all because of her because of my sister who clings to my head and won't fall off but honestly honestly to be really honest i dont want to hate anyone and i dont want to hit anyone i dont want to hurt anyone and i dont want anyone to hit anyone else i dont want to cause any trouble i dont want to do anything wrong i didnt do anything wrong this is all because of you its because of me i started i started drawing a weird triangle i drew three crooked lines and it turned into a weird triangle i put Rang and Washington Hat in and drew the lines of our weird triangle it—*

I get up from my seat.

A girl walks into the classroom. She looks at me. I don't know her name. I don't even care, but she keeps looking at me.

I walk out into the hallway.

The baseball team, the kids from my class, and the kids from the next classroom over are all in the hallway. There are younger kids, too. There are boys and girls. Only the teachers are missing. They're always missing. And as always, something bad is happening since the teachers are missing. I peer into the bad thing. This time, it's worse than it has ever been before, I think. I think that every day. Every day, it gets a little worse. Everyone knows that. How far will it go? That's what we all wonder. Our eyes grow big and our mouths disappear. Every day during lunch, without fail, a swarm of kids. They crowd into the hallway and silently peer in. The baseball boys move silently, and Rang's body shakes silently. And then there's me, watching. Just like everybody else. Washington Hat sees me and smiles. The smile is, as always, very cute. I want to touch his face. I want to hold it in my palm and stroke it. How I'd let myself be stroked like a dog, just to keep seeing that smile. But Washington Hat's smile quickly fades as he goes back to beating Rang. A large boy punching a small girl, as though mashing potatoes. It's not normal. We all know that, which is why we are watching. I'm really sick and tired of it. The same song keeps playing, but it's not a good song. It's quite horrible. I watch Washington Hat's face. His mouth is firmly shut. I hear a *thump*. For a very brief moment, time stops. Then it flows again. Slowly. Too slowly. The kids are still silent. I can't take it anymore. I don't want to listen to this song anymore.

I stretch my hand out to Washington Hat. He doesn't look up. I say: *I don't want to be with you anymore.*

It's suddenly quiet. I repeat—this time louder and

clearer—*I don't want to hang out with you anymore.*
Everybody has heard me this time. Washington Hat looks
at me. I look back at him. I say, *I'm not your dog. No one is
your dog here.*

Then I take the hat off and throw it out the window.
The hat flies out, everything stopping as it lands on the
ground.

18

I decide not to think about what happens next.

19

Now I really don't hang out with anyone. I don't hang
out with anyone because they're all boring. Of course, I'm
boring too, so being alone is enough. A group of dull
people would just make things even more miserable. I'm
like a dog. Dogs don't have friends. They only have own-
ers. That's all they need. What's the difference between
dogs and humans? I'll just live like a dog. I flip a page
in my textbook. We're in social studies. There's a map
drawn in the textbook. A map of someplace I've never
been. Next to the map is a picture of some people. They're
laughing. But that has nothing to do with me. *I'll be a dog.*
I reaffirm my decision. I like it. Yes. That's what I'll do. I
don't need friends. Rang: I don't like you. I glower at her
seat. She isn't here. She didn't come to school today. Not

having friends is amazing. It means I don't need to care if Rang comes to school or not. It means my iron weights get lighter. It means I can stay home and not expect anything. It means I don't have to hope. It's amazing to know in advance that things will just get worse, because there's no need to feel disappointed. Why, then, am I crying? I blink and a tear falls. The teardrop bursts as soon as it lands on my textbook. It turns into a dark stain, seeping into the paper. I put a finger on it. It's a little hot or a little cold. I turn another page. I grip my pen with all my strength. I shake my head and think, *it's okay*. The tear will soon dry and the dark stain will lighten. There's no need to worry.

20

I'm in agony and I'm getting even more boring.

21

Rang doesn't show up to school, but she shows up in my dreams.

22

The baseball boys got bored once Rang stopped coming to school. So did everyone else—it showed on their faces. We all needed a new Rang, it turned out. Getting bored is the worst thing that can happen to kids. Scarier than kicking your friend to death. We wanted a new Rang and got one quite easily: it was me. I was standing in the school hallway, watching the trees outside. They were lush and green. From my left, Washington Hat came toward me. Tokyo Hat approached from my right. Shanghai Hat stood watching me from beneath the lush trees. I didn't move. I didn't know what to do. I didn't realize what it meant.

"Ow!"

It wasn't me who shouted—it was Washington Hat. I looked at him. He was looking at me, his face distorted with pain. I didn't say anything. "Ow!" Washington Hat yelled again.

"What's going on?" I asked.

"Why did you hit me?" Washington Hat said.

"I didn't."

"Why did you hit me, huh?"

"When did I…"

Suddenly, Washington Hat grabbed my head and started shaking it. "Ow, ow!" I yelled. He shook my head harder. My body was jerked this way and that and then I fell to the ground. Washington Hat laughed. So did all the other Hats. The laughter grew fainter and fainter and then it died out completely. It was very quiet. Like nothing had happened at all. But I knew it wasn't over. This was the beginning.

I am not loved by my teachers. I know this because they don't do anything when the baseball boys hit me. I'm certain the baseball boys are more loved than me. And I know because every day the baseball boys' moms come to school and pick them up in cute white or red cars. My mom can't do that, because she doesn't have a car. She doesn't have a car because we don't have any money. It's disgusting. These thoughts are disgusting. But I'm not making anything up. I'm getting beaten up. Or, more like, I'm getting wrestled. Or, more like, I'm being stripped down. Or, more like, I'm being fondled. Washington Hat doesn't stroke me like I'm his dog anymore. He fondles me like I'm a naked Barbie doll. No, he doesn't fondle me. He nudges and rubs it against me. I can't help but think terrible thoughts when it's happening, about how I want to kill Washington Hat. I imagine what it would be like to kill him. But if I can it's better to not think at all when it's happening. It's better to stop altogether, like a clock with its batteries removed. It's better to slice out the time that is unfolding right now and pretend it doesn't exist. It's better to scoop the memories of this time out of my head. It's better to believe that I'm just having a bad dream. The real issue is stumbling home after a beating every day. But there's nothing else I can do. It's undeniable that everyone keeps their distance from me. I'm more alone than I've ever been. Killing Washington Hat would be easier than enduring this. What I'll do is hide a hammer in my backpack and sneak it into the school. After the bell rings, I'll stay put for about fifteen minutes, then leave the classroom with my bag. I'll quietly enter the classroom next door—Washington Hat's classroom. His seat is in the back row, on the far left. As I approach him, I'd quickly draw out the hammer, then hit him on the head with it. That's it. It'd be much easier than you might expect.

But I know I won't be able to do it. Washington Hat knows it, too. He knows that no one will do that to him. And, since we know and he knows, nothing will change, and Washington Hat will live. He'll live for a long, long time.

The kids, watching, are quiet.

What do you want? What do you want? Tell me, I'll do it.

Just tell me!

"Take off your shirt," Washington Hat says.

"Then I won't hit you."

Washington Hat smiles.

It's still cute.

Everyone is watching. My cheeks are wet. They're

smeared

all over with something.

Someone is talking, but I can barely hear what they're saying. My ears are covered. So is my mouth, it seems. No, not covered—I'm eating something. No, not eating—something's in it. In my mouth. No. On my palms, on the soles of my feet, something is clinging to me. No. In my hair, my eyebrows. It tickles. Between my toes. Something squirms. Something alive. Something alive crawls up from my foot. No. It crawls down. No. One crawls up and another crawls down. There are three, not two. My body shakes. No. It trembles. I'm cold. No. I'm sweating. No. I'm crying.

"Take your skirt off. Then I won't hit you."

"Take off your underwear. Then I won't hit you."

"Then I won't hit you," says Washington Hat, and then he hits me.

I can't
breathe.

Everyone is wearing a baseball cap.
The caps are all the same.
It's the middle of the day, I think, but everything's dark.
It's so dark that I can't see
any
of their faces.

My flesh is being stripped off—no, my stockings are?

My senses are vanishing—no, my skirt is?

My lips are torn—no, my bra is?

Why are you doing this to me!

Why?

It's because we're cowards.

We're cowards!

The cowards yell, and at the same time they stretch out toward a large hole. Everything streams into the hole. But I am the hole. Washington Hat smiles. *Still cute,* I think. I close my eyes, but I can still see Washington Hat's smile. It doesn't fade, but lingers in my mind. I don't want to kill Washington Hat anymore. I want to die. I want to die.

24

Rang opens her hands. The number seventeen is written on her palm. It's the seventeenth time that Rang has appeared in my dream. That's what she says, so it must be true. I don't know anything anymore. In my dream, Rang shows me her palm with the number seventeen on it for seventeen hours. For seventeen hours, I sit and look at Rang's open palm. Time goes by very slowly. My body moves very slowly as well. Rang's body starts to shine. It grows brighter and brighter, and the light eventually fills the whole room. I keep looking at Rang. Suddenly, I realize that we're in a hat. We are in Washington Hat's hat, squirming like little mice.

25

Eighteenth.

26

I didn't want to dream, so I started staying awake at night. I kept my eyes wide open, watching my sleeping parents and sister all night. Fortunately, my parents and sister slept very well. When the sun rose, I'd take my bag and go to school. The school was empty. I'd open a window, crawl into the nurse's office, and fall asleep. There weren't any dreams when I slept anymore. It was just bright and white, like the nurse's office. When I woke up and opened the door to go to class, the baseball boys would appear from everywhere and yank my hair. Even as they were dragging me by my hair, I would doze off again. I wasn't angry anymore. Just tired. Everything seemed like a dream. More and more of every day was spent in a dream. I saw Rang everywhere, and I didn't harass my sister anymore. Though sometimes I still wanted to kick her. But I was too sleepy to do it. Like melted cheese, I stuck to the floor, immobile. Stuck to the floor, I watched Rang slowly sway in front of me.

When I walked through the school gates, the baseball field swerved to the side. I started stumbling across the field in a zigzag. The baseball boys ran after me in a zigzag. But I was okay. Rang was with me. When I opened my eyes, I was still in the same place, zigzagging in the same place. Rang was with me, and the baseball kids were swarming.

Nobody was in the classroom when I opened the door. As soon as I walked in, I fell over and fell asleep.

In my dream, Rang spoke to me.

"I've decided not to show up in your dreams anymore, because I don't like you anymore."

We were crossing the field. The wind was blowing and twirled Rang's hair. I couldn't say anything to her.

"So this is our last time. Bye."

Rang started to drift away. In a zigzag. I floundered, trying to say, *no*, I think. And then I woke up.

When I woke up, my Korean teacher was looking down at me.

"Are you sick?"

"No."

"Then go back to your seat."

I did as she said, then almost jumped back up in surprise when I saw that Rang was sitting in the seat in front of mine. She gave me a little wave and I waved back.

"Sleepy?" she asked.

"Yeah."

Rang smiled. She looked so happy. It was weird; I didn't feel happy at all.

"Rang, I don't like you."

When I said that, Rang replied: "Yeah, I don't like you either."

And then she disappeared, just like that. I opened my eyes again, and we were back on the baseball field.

Rang said, "I've decided not to show up in your dreams anymore, because I don't like you anymore."

We were crossing the field. The wind was blowing and twirled Rang's hair. I couldn't say anything to her.

"So this is our last time. Bye."

Again, I woke up. I lifted my head and saw the Korean teacher looking down at me.

"Are you sick?"

"Yes."

"Then go to the nurse's office."

I stood up and all the kids turned to look at me. Rang wasn't there, but it felt like she might be hiding somewhere, watching me. Under the teacher's desk, hanging out of the hallway window, inside a locker. Too frightened to stay in the classroom any longer, I hurried out. Rang wasn't anywhere. But I knew she was lurking nearby, hiding and spying on me. Why? To harass me! I ran down the stairs. On the way, I saw the baseball boys through the window. I crossed the baseball field in a straight line. This time, they didn't chase me. I slipped through the gates and Rang wasn't there. I crossed the street and passed the alley. Still, Rang was nowhere, even when I reached my house. I opened the door and saw my sister. Like always, she was lying on the floor. For some reason, she looked a little green. I looked down at my slightly green sister.

Her eyes were closed, but she didn't seem to be sleeping. I gathered her in my arms. She writhed, with her green face and green breath.

"It's okay," I whispered. "It's okay. It's okay. It's okay." And then I closed my eyes and fell asleep, a little bit, a little bit at a time.

28

When I opened my eyes again, the sun was setting. It was a fiery red, as though setting the whole world on fire. The window was wide open, and the dense smell of soy sauce poured in with the sunset. My sister was sleeping like a corpse in the corner. I stood and went to the window. The bright red sunset looked as though it were swallowing the factory. It really was something. It was so immense and spooky that I felt like the whole world would disappear with the sun.

I closed the window.

My sister was still lying in the corner. She hadn't moved, but she seemed greener than before. I turned the television on and sat on the floor. The television showed a burning mountain—the mountain was green, like my sister. And the fire was red, like the sunset. A helicopter flew through the air, spraying white over all of it. I looked at my sister. Her green had gotten darker. So dark it was practically black. I shook my head. *Am I dreaming? Maybe I haven't woken up yet?* I turned the television off and called out to her.

She didn't reply.

"Hey, wake up. I'm hungry. Make some ramyeon."

She was silent.

"Hey, wake up! I said, make some ramyeon."

I stretched my hand out to touch her. And as soon as it touched her body, I froze. Immediately, everything turned green, anything and everything within my sight. The ceiling, the floor, the television, and my sister—everything. I couldn't tell what was my sister and what wasn't. Nothing moved and everything was silent. Only the green changed, growing darker and darker. The longest second in the world passed. I forced my mouth open. A thin sound leaked out. It grew louder and louder and eventually became a scream. I covered my ears and ran.

29

This is a dream. No, it's not. Yes, it is. No! But it's what you wanted, right? Do you really want it to be a dream? No? I don't know! I want to see the ocean. I want to dive into the waves. I want to go in and never come out. That's what I'm going to do. I'm gonna do it. I'll never come back out of the water. Never come back. Never. I'm going to turn into a fish! Yes.

I'll be a fish!

The sky was getting dark. The seagulls flying in circles looked like a school of fish. The streets were cooling into a blue hue. The colors of sand and waves mixed with the wind. The moon and the stars hid behind the clouds, out of sight. In the far distance, I could see a dim glimmer of blinking lights. The sound of the waves whispered to me. The smell of the ocean thickened. The clouds draped across the sky were still, as though dead. The ocean was getting closer and closer. And I was running. My face layered with sweat and tears. As soon as I jumped into the water, I realized that I wasn't alone, that I had company. It was Rang.

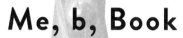

Me, b, Book

I'm just experimenting.

No, you're crazy and you're trying to kill yourself.

That's not it. I just want to know.

Know what?

Exactly how desperate I can be.

1

We went to the End.

2

I was watching the sea. Golden birds flew over the red-tinged sea. A faraway boat swayed in black shadows. The crimson waves shook the sea as they rippled. I made up my mind: *I won't go back to school. No, I won't do anything. Just like Book.* I turned to look behind me. Book was sitting on the sand, reading. He read with his neck stretched toward the book as though trying to climb into it. "There are all sorts of books in the world," Book once said. "Because all sorts of people write all sorts of books. They're all about the world outside the book, which means all things start outside the book but end up within a book. That's what I want. I want to go into books." That's what Book had said when we were at his house, eating ramyeon. Book had continued: "All I do is read. I don't do anything else. I don't write reviews. I'm not inspired to draw or sing. I don't get smarter or broader or narrower. I don't become deeper or shallower. I don't become more of an adult or more childlike. I don't become more abundant or barren. That's the true way to read books, I think. Most people read to learn something new. Or to gain something: to get smarter, to transform or be transformed, to be different, to reflect, to remember, to grow deeper, get better or worse. They read to shake off boredom or sadness, or they read to be sad, or bored, or happy; to be unhappy, to be angry or hold back anger, to forgive or not forgive, to cry, to dry their tears. They read because they're afraid. But I'm not afraid. I came out here to really read books. I don't know anyone here, I don't know this city, and I don't care about it. I don't want to know anything about it—I just want to read. People say it's not healthy to do nothing except read. They say I should do something else. They say I should watch movies, meet people, eat good food. I should wonder about this city, this country, and this world that I live in. But I don't agree with them. No, I don't want to do any of that. I wish everyone would leave me alone. I don't care where I live or if the country changes its name tomorrow or if the world comes to an end. Everything is always the same anyway. People are born and people die. In between, they eat. They eat so they won't die. That's it. So, it really doesn't matter to me whether I eat ramyeon or bread. I just need books. People think I'm like this because I'm crazy. But I think they're just as crazy as I am. Everyone is crazy. Out of their minds. That's why I don't like people. I don't like myself, either. I just like books."

The ocean finally swallowed the sinking sun. Then the ocean grew red like the sun had been, like Book. "That's it," Book said. I looked at him again. He wasn't reading; he was looking at the ocean. "There's a painting I once saw," Book said, "a painting of a man without any clothes on. With both hands he was holding a bathroom sink and his head was shoved into it. The man was trying to climb into the sink. I was so surprised when I saw it, because that man was me. I try to get into books like that man was trying to go into the sink drain. Yes. I want to go *inside* books. That's my dream. I want to go in and never come out." After saying that, Book fell silent. I looked back toward the ocean. It was now black. The sky was black, too. So were the seagulls. Everything had turned into a shadow. Book turned on a flashlight and shined it at the sky. And then he started reading again. I thought about the drain in the bathroom sink. It must be a very sad painting. No doubt, a painting that said *Iwouldrathergointothebathroomsinkdrain* was even sadder than a painting that said *Iwouldratherdie*. Flipping a page in his book, Book's shoulders hunched even more. I didn't want to go down a drain in a bathroom sink. I didn't want to disappear into a book, either. I wanted to be swallowed by the ocean. That sounded good enough for me. That's exactly how desperate I was. If going into the sink is a hundred percent desperate, I was maybe around seventy. If being swallowed by the sea is a hundred percent desperate, going inside a book would be about 120 percent. Yes, that much desperation. I'd have to be 120 percent desperate to put even a single finger within a book. But 120 percent is impossible. I might be able to

I said it's beginning.

This is hard.

No, it's easy.

Hard.

No, it's easy. It just feels hard because you're going crazy.

Maybe that's true.

Go home.

Why?

That's how you can return to normal.

Are you saying I'm not normal right now?

You're thinking about walking into the ocean.

I'm just experimenting.

No, you're crazy and you're trying to kill yourself.

That's not it. I just want to know.

Know what?

Exactly how desperate I can be.

But...

I don't think Book is crazy. He's just making a wish. A wish that can't come true. He's just waiting for a miracle.

That's why he's crazy.

I want to be that desperate.

Why?

I want to be the ocean.

You're going to be a junior in high school.

No, I'm not going back to school ever again.

Stop. Stop walking into the ocean.

No.

You're going to die.

No, I'm going to become the ocean.

No, you have to be a junior.

Why?

Because. Listen to me: It's easy, just go back home. It's simple.

No, it's complicated. It's hard.

You'll go back soon.

"No!" I yelled.

"No! I'm not going home! I won't be a junior! I'm going to be the ocean!"

The water was already up to my thighs. I kept moving forward. The water soon swallowed my butt, then my waist, and soon it touched my arms. Then the water clenched my chest and my neck. I stopped and looked back. Book was far away. I took another step. The water swallowed my nose. I blinked. I have to be more desperate. The water swallowed my eyes. I took another step. Suddenly, something collapsed beneath my feet. I lost my balance and fell; I immediately began to sink, as though someone was pulling me down from below. Instead of thrashing around, I closed my eyes and thought about desperation. But all I did was sink deeper. I…I couldn't be more desperate than I was now. I started crying. My tears mixed with the ocean. The ocean covered me like a thick blanket and pulled me in. I can't. I can't hang on anymore. And then something soft touched my body. And I floated. A faint light got closer. A moment later, I emerged from the water. I opened my eyes. b's face was in front of me. 120 percent. A miracle.

3

One hundred and twenty percent, Rang said. And then she spilled over me.

4

b was crying. The waves crashed over her wet face. Everything was like b's tears. I held her hands tight. Book was running toward us. b also held my hands tight. And we escaped from the sea.

5

When I opened the door to Highway Grocery, a large white dog came up, wagging its tail. Water was dripping from our clothes. Light peeked from the gap of a door beyond the dusty shelves. The door opened, and the dark, wet floor shone with light.

While we wiped our bodies with the rags the old lady gave us, Book paced in the front of the grocery. She gave us hot barley tea. I could see a plastic bag dangling from Book's arm. The faint sound of the television came from the back room.

"Why are you so wet? Did you fall in the ocean?" asked the old lady.

We held the cups of hot barley tea with two hands and blew on them.

"And why isn't he wet?" she asked, looking at Book.

"He was reading," I said.

"What?"

"I said, he was reading."

"Idiot," said the old lady.

b burst out laughing.

"Why are you laughing?"

"She called him an idiot!" b said, still laughing.

I began to laugh too, and so did the old lady. I felt better as my body got warm. We kept laughing and I felt better and better. *Achoo.* b sneezed. We kept laughing.

6

"Are both of you really going to run away from home?" Book asked.

We didn't answer, sitting on a chair together.

My leg hurt. Book made a fist and massaged his knee, which made him look like an old man. I looked at b. She was also holding back a laugh.

Achoo! b sneezed again.

"Are you getting sick?" Book asked.

"No," b said, shaking her head.

"You're lying."

"She's not," I said. *Achoo.* b had sneezed again.

"That's bad." Book made a fist.

"Why?" I asked.

"I really hate being sick."

"Me too," said b, then rubbed her nose with her left hand.

"You can't really read books when you're sick."

"Why not?"

"Because your head keeps spinning." Book made a spinning motion with his hand next to his head.

"Then just don't read," said b. Book glared at her and she glared back.

"You…" Book started to say. "Never mind. Forget it."

"What? Say it."

"You're quite bold." Book covered his mouth and laughed, *hee hee hee.*

b burst out laughing.

"What, what's so funny?"

"You," said b.

"What about me?"

"Hee hee." b mimicked Book's laugh. I bit my lips and looked down.

"The bus!" We looked in the direction he had pointed. There wasn't anything there, and we looked back at Book. "Just joking, it isn't coming… Hee…"

Book had started to laugh again, but then he glanced at b and closed his mouth.

"Why are you looking at me like that?" b said, holding back her laughter. "You can laugh as much as you want."

Book waved his hand as if waving off a fly.

b started laughing again.

"Why do you keep laughing? Why?!"

"You're super funny," b said, clutching her stomach.

Book looked at me as if asking me to help.

"Stop it," I said. "He's embarrassed."

"Oh…seriously?" b stopped laughing and took her

hands off her stomach. "I'm sorry."

"Whatever."

"No, I'm really sorry."

"I said, whatever!"

"Okay, well then."

"Are we going to take the bus?" I asked.

"Yeah, is there a problem?"

"I don't have any money for the bus," I said.

"Me neither," b said.

"Are you asking me to pay your fare?"

"We're not asking you to just pay. We're asking to borrow it," b said.

"Hmm…"

Book shook his head, putting his hand to his forehead.

"You can't pay for us?" b asked.

"It's okay. You take the bus and we'll just walk," I said.

"It's not that! I have more than enough money!" Book yelled, then took money out of his pocket and handed us each some. It was crumpled up thousand-won bills.

"I can pay your fare anytime!"

I looked at b, who still looked amused. Book shook his head. There was the faint sound of an engine. It was the bus. We stood as the bus slowly came to a stop, and we all got on together.

7

The bus stopped at the northern edge of the city. It was the last stop, and we were the last ones on the bus. As the empty bus drove away, Book took a flashlight from a plastic bag. We crossed the road and slipped into the woods. In the pitch-dark forest, Book moved as swift as a squirrel. b kept sneezing.

"How much farther do we have to go?" I asked.

"We're here."

And with one more step, Book simply disappeared. Surprised, we ran to where he had been. The forest fell away and there was Book. Around him on the ground were a million sparks, but it wasn't dust. They were stars. *Wow!* b exclaimed. In the blink of an eye, time had stopped. And then it slowly returned and flowed again. *I won't forget this*, I thought. And that's true. I still remember everything, all of it.

8

b first, then me, then Book got sick.

9

Achoo. b wiped her nose and threw the tissue on the floor. Then she collapsed onto the bed. "Ouch!" Book yelled, sticking his head out from under the blankets and glaring at her. I was wedged between the bed and the wall. The flu had conquered my nose and my neck, and was rolling around in my forehead. I was freezing. "I'm hungry," b mumbled weakly. I sniffled. Book crawled out from under the blankets. b and I started fighting over them. Book's face was red with fever. He put on three sweaters and started making thick porridge. Book's cramped house was soon filled with heat from the boiling porridge. It was like the inside of a thick, wet cotton blanket.

"I'm hot," I said.

"Yeah, it's too hot," b said.

"No, it's chilly," Book said. But we ignored him and opened the door. Book shrieked and closed it again. The porridge overflowed. "Whoa!" The expression on Book's face as he dashed to the pot was ridiculous. He turned off the stove and collapsed on the floor. Dripping with sweat, b and I crawled to the pot. *We look like idiots*, I thought. The three of us, red-faced and shivering, *we look like idiots*.

10

That night, the night our flus were the worst, we suffered until dawn. Book had made pitiful animal noises for an hour. b had been quiet, as though dead. Rolling to my left, I could see crumpled up tissues, bowls, bits of trash, and pots with dried porridge inside. *I'm hungry*, I thought. Strawberries tumbled from the sky like magic. Wow. I stretched out my hand to the falling strawberries, but each one that hit my hand was hot and painful. I shrieked and crawled under the blankets. b was sitting at the edge of the bed. Her face as white as milk, she began talking:

"I dreamed that my sister died. My mom and dad and I were burying her. My mom was digging, my dad, too. I kept watch. It was a freezing winter night, and my breath was white in the air. The pile of dirt grew higher as the hole grew deeper. My mom grabbed my sister's legs and my dad grabbed her head. I grabbed somewhere around her middle. *One, two, three.* We threw her in the hole. My mom started to cry, my dad lit a cigarette, and I took a tangerine out of my pocket. But it was green, like my sister had been. Surprised, I threw it into the hole as well. 'We have to hurry,' my mom said. My dad nodded and we began to fill up the hole. As the sun began to rise, the hole was nearly filled. The police were coming. My mom and dad ran away without me. 'Mom!' I shouted. 'Dad!' But they were already gone. I was alone. Crying, I began to run too. The police were chasing me. I tried to run faster, but I slipped and fell into the sea. My sister was looking down at me from above the water. The police were looking down at me, too. Rang—you were looking at me too. And Book, and my mom and dad, everyone. But you were all green. I didn't know what to do, and I was sinking."

I said: "In my dream, I wanted to eat strawberries. But I was winter. I was a cold and poor winter. I couldn't eat strawberries. I had no choice but to go in the ocean, but the ocean was so cold; it was frozen, so I couldn't swim in it. No one could swim. People didn't know what a wave or fish was. Instead, they had gotten very good at ice-skating, because they skated all day. They hunted penguins for food. There were a hundred types of penguin dishes. Penguin fried rice, penguin sandwiches, penguin noodles, penguin cookies, penguin stew, a hundred recipes and they were all very good. Except I wanted strawberries! Every morning, though, I had to eat penguin soup with penguin bread. Every night, I dreamed about penguins screaming and begging for me to save them. I couldn't sleep. I woke up crying. All I wanted was to eat strawberries."

"But I couldn't do anything," said b. "My sister was so green. I hated her. I hated her so much and I couldn't cry." b started crying. "I hated my sister so much. I didn't love her. I was cruel to her. Which is why I sank of course!" b yelled. She sounded like the screaming penguins. "But my sister was green! I was so scared. She had a disease that had turned her into a leaf. And it was all because of me. I threw away her medicine. I told her to make me ramyeon. I kicked her. When she was sleeping, I prayed that she'd hurry up and die!

"I kicked my sick sister!" b yelled. "That's why she died!"

As b screamed, I tumbled back down into my dream, full of strawberries. I picked one up to eat it, but it started talking. Looking closely, I realized it wasn't a strawberry, but Book. No, just someone who looked a lot like Book. It was his brother. "Does my brother still read all the time?" he asked. Book's brother was beige. *Book's brother is beige*, I muttered. I was still inside my dream and b was with me. No, she *was* me, too. Book's brother was calling out, but suddenly, I tumbled into b's dream. But b's dream was Book's dream. And their dreams were actually my dream. We all fell into a single dream together, and then we were split into three dreams. Everything was mixed up, which meant that we could do anything. b buried her sister five more times. She threw her into the sea, burned her, even tied a rope around her waist and dragged her. Book read an illustrated book about plants. I became the purple flower in the book. Book was lying in a field of purple flowers. The wind blew and Book pulled out his itchy eye. It was a ball, which Washington Hat hit with his bat. The ball flew far and rolled. White snow landed on it. The snow became the foam from a wave. The foam became white snow again, and we were suddenly in the middle of winter at the North Pole. b was a polar bear. I was a fish, and the polar bear grabbed me. She put me in her mouth. The inside of her mouth was shiny. There were stars in its sky. Smoke rose—it was the chimney of the factory. Someone was dangling from the chimney: b's sister. She was green and dying. I started to climb the chimney as people clapped and cheered me on. I crawled toward b's sister, who was Book, hanging from metal chains. I was b, crawling toward my sister. b's heart was so sad. It hurt, so I couldn't climb very well. I started to cry and tears fell from b's eyes. They fell onto Book's green cheeks. Book didn't move. I was hurting. It hurt so much. But the pain was b's. b was punching the bed. She sobbed and punched the bed. I held her hand, but she tore it away. "I deserve to drown!" She punched the bed. The house trembled and books fell from the ceiling. Book picked up a book that had fallen. It was a dictionary. Book opened it. The word *rendezvous* was written in big letters inside. *Rendezvous. Two or more spacecrafts meeting in a docking station.* Book read in a loud voice: "Rendezvous: Two or more space-crafts meeting in a docking station." "This is a dream," b said. "In this dream, I'm in space. I'm a spaceship. I'm

Fever.

Headache.

Sneeze.

Snot.

Fever.

Fever.

Fever.

Cold.

No, hot.

Cold.

No, hot.

Cold.

No, hot!

No, cold!

Hot!

I'm hot!

We're sick.

We're sick.

We're sick!

All three of us opened our eyes at once. We were lying in the bed, under a single blanket. Only thirty minutes had passed. The house hadn't shaken once. b hadn't gone to space. I didn't want to eat strawberries. We were just suffering from the flu. I heard a bird singing faintly. Bluish light seeped under the door. I put my hand to my forehead. It wasn't hot. It wasn't sweaty, either. I rubbed my eyes. I stood and walked in a straight line. It was possible. I opened the door.

Light, bright morning light, poured in.

I put a foot outside. My toes touched the grass. It didn't hurt. Dew covered the grassy field. I breathed in. The air was new.

I'm not sick anymore, I thought.

Yes, that was true.

11

I was incredibly hungry.

12

Book brought out his biggest pot. It was so big b and I could wear it on our heads together, at the same time. So we did.

"Hee hee!" Book laughed as he watched us. He was standing with his back to the sun, so he looked like a silhouette cut from a black piece of paper.

"Hee hee!"

"Why do you keep laughing like that?" I asked.

"How are you supposed to laugh?"

"*Hahaha,*" b said. "Laugh like this: *Hahaha.*"

"I *did* laugh like that!" Book was getting upset.

"Liar! You laughed like this: *Hee hee.*"

"Did not!"

"Liar!"

"I did not!"

"Then laugh again. *Hahaha*, like that."

"Hmm… Book cleared his throat. Then he sneaked a glance at us before laughing very quietly and quickly and softly.

"Teeheehee."

"Oh my gosh." b shook her head. "That's *teehee*."

Book's face turned red.

"You don't know how to laugh: *Hahaha*."

"I do know." But Book's voice sounded weak.

"I don't think so."

"Whatever! Stop it! I won't laugh!" Book shouted angrily. "I won't laugh again! I won't!"

Book stomped over to us, his face angry. Then he reached out his arm, very quickly. Surprised, we pulled back, gasping. He snatched the pot off our heads, then went to the kitchen and poured water into it. I looked at b.

"You were too hard on him."

"Was I?"

"Yes."

"But it was funny."

"That's true."

We lay on the floor. "Damn it," Book muttered. "Damn it, damn it," he muttered over and over as he put the pot on the stove.

"When's your birthday?" I asked him.

"January 1st."

"Whoa," I exclaimed.

"Whoa," said b.

13

Hoo. b blew on the ramyeon.

Hoo. Book blew on the ramyeon.

Hoo. I blew on the ramyeon.

14

"Oh, I'm so full." b lay on the ground and patted her stomach.

"Yeah, me too." I lay on the ground and patted my stomach as well.

"You'll get a stomachache if you lie down after eating," Book said, lying on the ground and pulling out a book.

"That's okay," we said. And then we fell asleep.

15

The next morning, we ate ramyeon again.

"When are you two going back home?" Book asked.

We didn't respond.

That evening, we ate ramyeon again.

The next morning, we ate ramyeon yet again. It was beginning to taste a little worse.

That night, we ate ramyeon again. It was just alright.

"Do you only eat ramyeon?" b asked.

"No," Book said. "I'm not unhealthy, I just ran out of other food."

"Then you should go to the store."

"You realize you're asking for a lot of free food?"

"That's…"

Book checked the clock. "Oh!"

"What?"

"I have to be somewhere." Book stood up.

"Where?"

"Why do you care?"

"Okay, don't tell us if you don't want to," said b.

Book shook his head.

And then, with the face of someone revealing a huge secret, he said: "I go grocery shopping with the Alone guy."

"Cool, I want to go, too," b said.

"Me too," I added.

"No!"

"Why not?"

Book looked at us. We made pitiful faces. He grimaced, like he didn't know what to do.

"Damn it." Book shook his head.

16

We went to the bus station and waited for the owner of Alone. Book had a black plastic bag in one hand and held the handle of a large shopping cart in the other. b kept poking the cart and giggling. Every now and then something blinked in the dark woods across the street. I held b's hand.

"It's cold," I mumbled.

Cars with headlights on zoomed past us from both directions. Each time one passed, my hair swung from left to right or right to left. A white car approached—in the dark it looked like a ghost. It slowed, then stopped in front of Book. He opened the door. It smelled like cigarettes. We climbed in.

17

The road stretched straight ahead, just like the trees that stretched their arms straight toward the sun. The light from the streetlights was faint and white. We were the only ones on the road. The city, now far behind us, held the high, dense sky on its shoulders. On either side of the road, a vast and empty field stretched out endlessly. The sky was as dark as it was wide and there were scarcely any stars to be seen. Occasionally, a few low buildings appeared, but they disappeared immediately. Book was reading and the owner of Alone kept his mouth shut. Songs as pale and tired as dusk played from the radio. Then an apartment complex came into view. Huge apartment buildings spread to the end of the world. In the center sat a big low building with its lights on. The supermarket.

The owner of Alone parked near the market and stepped out of the car to smoke. Book stayed in the car, but b and I got out to roam around. "Don't go too far!" the owner of Alone shouted. We stopped in our tracks. A crouched cat was glowering at us. It was black and white. The cat smoothly lifted its body, took a few steps, sprung over a fence, and disappeared. We returned to the car. The owner of Alone had stubbed out his cigarette.

As soon as we entered the supermarket, the owner of Alone filled his cart. Book's cart held nothing but a bottle of coke, roasted seaweed, and chicken. "Get something else," the owner of Alone said, clapping Book on the shoulder. b fell asleep in a cart I was pushing around. She had grabbed a bag of cinnamon bears. I pushed the cart slowly and looked at all the products. The owner of Alone was standing in front of some hiking boots. We passed him and went to the goldfish. They were swimming around slowly, looking bored. We passed the fish counter and it smelled like old, rotting ocean. "I want to go back to the ocean," I said quietly. b's eyes were still closed, and her body shook a little as the cart moved. I heaved the shopping cart forward and let go. It slid on and on with incredible speed. It passed the cookies, coffee, and tea, finally stopping in front of the sugars. But b still didn't move. Neither did I—I stood still, watching the cart with b in it.

18

"Do you think you're an adult?" I asked Book.

He shook his head, and the owner of Alone burst out laughing.

We were at Alone. Alone's owner was making coffee, and the rest of us were seated around a small table in the corner. The only light came from the bar, and a tango played from the speakers. b was messing with the sugar bowl.

"Do I seem like an adult to you?" Book asked.

"No." I shook my head.

Book nodded. "I see."

"No, that is, I mean…" Book stared at me silently. b and the owner of Alone did, too. I could feel my face going red. "You're old enough to be an adult."

"He is," the owner of Alone added, smiling.

"But you don't seem like an adult."

"So?" Book asked.

"She's saying you're ridiculous," b said.

"No," I said.

"Are you saying I'm pathetic?" Book asked.

"Yes," said b.

"No," I answered.

"It's not like that. Whatever. Forget I said anything."

The owner of Alone laughed as he poured coffee into a mug.

"By the way, shouldn't you two go home?" the owner of Alone asked.

b and I didn't reply.

"Are you ever going back home?"

"I don't know. I'm not thinking about it," I said.

"I'm not going back," said b.

"Not now…" I said.

"But…"

"When I go to school, the boys beat me up for no reason. Why should I go back?"

"My mom doesn't care if I do my homework or not. Why should I go back?"

"I don't care about good grades and success like

Glasses. Why should I go back?"

"My only friend is b, and she's right here next to me. Why should I go back?"

"You're an adult, but you don't work, you're not married, and all you do is read. Tell us why we should go back."

"Because you're not adults yet," the owner of Alone said.

"So once we're adults we won't need to go back?"

"That's right."

"Then why does everyone call you crazy? Why do they say you two are pathetic? Why do they tell us not to end up like you?"

"What?"

"Pathetic? Us?"

"I'm crazy?"

"Yes. Everyone says so. That's why you live in the forest. They say you went crazy and went to live in the forest to read all day."

Book thought for a moment, then waved his left hand. "Let them think whatever they want."

"We…" said the owner of Alone gravely. "We're just a little different."

"Us too," said b.

"How?"

"My sister is dead."

19

"What do you think?"

"Do you think we should go back?"

20

"Not my problem," Book shrugged, "I don't care about worldly affairs."

I smiled.

"What?"

"I kind of like you."

21

"What?"

"Nothing bad will happen."

"I promise."

22

We left Alone as the sun began to rise. It was full morning by the time we arrived at Book's house. We ate ramyeon again and then fell asleep. It was lunch-time when we woke up. We boiled the chicken and ate it. Afterward, we were sleepy again. Book read, and b and I went back to bed. It was dinnertime when we got up. Book was still reading. We nagged him to cook, and he fried the leftover chicken with chili powder and soy sauce. We mixed it into rice. It was very good. After dinner, it was dark. Book resumed reading, and b and I fell back asleep.

23

A few days passed. Or maybe a few hours.

24

Book was lying on the bed reading. I was scribbling, leaning against a bookshelf. b was plucking grass and rolling around in the field. Book's house smelled of books. Floors, potatoes, and pots all smelled like books. I put the pen down and lay on the floor, wiggling my fingers and toes. It was a very quiet, very pleasant time. Everything seemed far away. School, the city, my mom, and even getting beaten up by Washington Hat. How many days had passed?

Book was still reading.

Reading in his black clothes, he resembled a large black rock. He looked so cool that I wanted to become a rock, too. But my skin felt like jelly. Too pale and limp to be rock.

I'm more like a squid.

I had a dream, Book said. But he said it so suddenly and casually that it sounded more like a hallucination or something. So I didn't respond.

Book repeated: "I had a dream."

"What did you say?"

"I said, I had a dream."

"What about?"

"I don't remember. But it was important."

"Try to remember."

"I am trying." Book looked at me, his eyes shining.

"Your eyes are shining," I said.

"Are they?"

"Yes."

"Speaking of which…" Book put down the book. "I'm thinking of going to the hospital today."

"The hospital?"

"That's right."

"What hospital?"

"It's not a real hospital. We just call it a hospital."

"What do you mean?"

"I can't explain it."

"Can I come with you?"

"No."

"Why not?"

Book was looking at me, and I made the most pitiful face I could muster. He was at a loss for words.

"Damn it." Book bowed his head.

25

Dinner that night was boiled potatoes. While we ate, Book rushed around, brushing his teeth and changing his clothes. After he was dressed, he stuffed a bunch of books into his bag. He kept taking one out and replacing it with another. He replaced each one again and again.

"What is he doing?" b whispered to me.

"I don't really know," I replied. "But he's definitely

going to a hospital." I drank some milk.

"Pass me the milk," said b. She tossed the last potato into her mouth.

Book zipped up his bag. Then he sneaked a glance at us.

I passed the milk to b, who gulped it down hurriedly.

It was dark outside. A large bag hung from Book's shoulder, and he had a black plastic bag dangling from his wrist. We quickly crossed the field and went into the woods. It was completely black inside the forest. Book turned on his flashlight. I held b's hand tight. It was so dark I couldn't tell if my eyes were open or closed. The flashlight showed occasional leaves that looked white and faded, and all I could hear was the sound of our breaths. A sudden fear swept over me. *Is that heavy breathing I hear next to me really b's?* I glanced in her direction and could barely make out her short, swaying hair. "Whoa!" b shouted suddenly. I turned to see a large old white building below us. There was something written over its doors. *City Metal Hospital.* The *n* in the middle was missing. "City Mental Hospital," b corrected aloud. Book started to run down the hill smoothly, as though sliding.

26

We didn't need to ask to know that the crowd in the hospital consisted entirely of people from the End. b and I hesitated, but Book strode forward into the crowd. Completely alone, b and I were terrified. And then we gradually began to get comfortable, because no one paid any attention to us. In a corner, some kids around our age wearing disgusting clothes were smoking with grave expressions. I approached them. One of them cursed and spat on me. Her saliva landed on my shirt and dripped down. Not knowing what to do, I kept still. The girl who had spit on me said, "Fuck off, bitch," which made me laugh. Then she said, "What're you laughing at, bitch?" Her hair was half blonde and half black. There were plastic necklaces dangling from her neck, as well as more plastic around her wrists and ankles. She was dark and thin like a spider. As I took a step toward her, she stepped back. My shirt still had her saliva clinging to it.

"What do you want, bitch?" She said.

"Don't swear at me," I said. She laughed with the kids next to her.

"Fuck off," she said.

"You going to hit me if I don't?"

b pulled at my arm. "No, let go." I brushed her hand away and took another step toward the girl. Her back was against the wall, so she couldn't back up anymore.

"Don't spit. And don't swear at people."

She looked at me with wide eyes. I smacked her lightly on the side of the head.

She didn't move, eyes still wide.

"It's irritating."

"Okay."

She agreed so easily that I was taken aback.

"I said okay, now fuck off."

I hesitated, but then turned to leave. At that moment, b shouted as the girl climbed onto my back. I fell to the ground and she began pulling at both of my ears. I struggled and was able to kick her in the stomach. "Oof," she yelled, falling flat on the ground. I didn't know what to do. b was stunned. The girl burst out crying. I looked back and forth from the girl to b. The other kids just watched her cry as well. The grown-ups in the crowd didn't even look at her. The plastic necklaces dangling from her neck jostled together and made clattering noises.

"Are you okay?" b asked.

"Yeah."

"Your hair is all tangled."

"It's okay."

"Let's go."

"Okay."

We just kept standing there for a long time though. The girl continued to cry, and the cigarettes between the fingers of the other kids slowly burned.

27

It had been a hospital, but it was not one now. It was unclear what it was currently used for. b said it looked like a dump. I said it looked like a factory. b said it looked like school. I said it looked like a playground. We pushed through the crowd and went up to the very top floor. It was quiet and empty there, except for the faint sound of voices if you listened very carefully. b placed her ear against one door after the next, following the sound. I looked out the window and saw the black forest.

"Come here," b called to me.

She was standing in front of a door at the very end of the corridor. It was open, and light spilled out. I came over.

"Whoa," I exclaimed quietly. The room was full of books. Many more than at Book's house. And, of course, Book was there.

There were other people besides him. They looked completely different than the people gathered outside the building. They were all young and wore normal clothes. Book and a person in a white outfit were bent over a desk covered in books.

"I had a dream yesterday…" Book said as our eyes met. "You came."

"Why did you leave us behind?" I said.

b didn't say anything.

"What was the dream about?" The person in white asked.

"I dreamed I became a book."

"Are you serious?"

"Yeah."

"What book?" the person in white asked.

"Yeah, tell us more," a person in green said.

"The cover was green. And…"

"Your name was written in every color, right?"

"Yeah."

"Page 367 said go northeast?"

"Yeah."

"67 kilometers?"

"Exactly."

"Congratulations," the person in green said. "It's completely accurate."

"Then how much more do I have left to do?" Book asked.

"I don't know. How long has it taken so far?" the person in green asked.

"I'm not sure," Book shrugged. "Three years?"

"Less than that," the person in white said. "It won't take that long."

"That's a relief. It's been hard." Book sighed heavily. At that moment, b screamed. A person in red had grabbed her.

"Who are you?"

"It's okay, leave them alone," Book said.

"Do you know them?"

"Yes. I mean, no. I mean, yeah, I know them."

"Do you know them or not?"

"I do. I know them."

The person in red looked disapproving as he let go of b, who rushed over to me.

"This isn't a place for you two."

"Why not?"

"Go home."

"No."

The person in red sighed.

"At least just go to the basement," the person in green said.

"Yeah, go to the basement," Book said.

"No, I won't," b said.

The people in green, white, and red all sighed at once.

"Fine, we'll be in the basement. Come get us when you're done with all this," I said.

"Sure, okay," Book answered half-heartedly.

b swore. The people in white, green, and red all turned and looked at her.

"Goodbye!" I yelled loudly as I took b's hand and left.

"Book, I hate you!" b shouted.

Laughter came from the room. b was heaving with anger. We started down the stairs. The smell of pee and something burning wafted over us. "Ugh." b retched. "What's that smell?"

"I don't know."

"Is there a fire?"

"But nobody's running away."

"It's because they're all crazy." b stopped.

"Let's see what's downstairs," I said.

"No. I'm not going down there." b was adamant. I had stopped as well. Nearby, a man stood, watching us. He wore a straw hat and looked nice enough.

"What's going on downstairs?"

"I don't know. It's my first time here." The man smiled.

"Then let's go down together." The man held my hand. I held b's. b grumbled that she didn't want to go, but she eventually surrendered. The smell thickened as we went downward. We held each other's hands tight and slowly felt our way down the stairs. We realized the reason for the smoke when we reached the basement. At the bottom of the stairs, a huge fan was blowing the smoke from some burning branches upward.

"Why are they doing this?" I asked the man.

"How would I know?" The man laughed.

"What brought you here, by the way?"

"Well, I don't know." The man laughed again. He seemed crazy.

"Hey, let's keep going by ourselves," b said.

"Okay." I let go of the man's hand. He was still laughing. I bid him farewell. "Bye, then."

"Sure, okay." The man smiled, and still smiling he drifted away.

There was a set of open doors behind the fan, with "Conversation Room" written above the doorway. It reeked of smoke and the scent of burning cinnamon. It stung—b had tears in her eyes. "I'm dizzy," I said. Two large fans slowly revolved in the ceiling. There were sparkly things attached to their blades. There were people lying on the floor, and other people simply walked over them. The people on the floor didn't make any noise. "Look over there," b said, and pointed. The owner of Alone was there, dancing with a girl wearing a gaudy pink wig. "Do you know who she is?" b asked. I told her I didn't. "I do," b said. "It's the youngest daughter of the family that owns Seoul Restaurant." Suddenly, I realized I was hungry. The youngest daughter of the family that owned Seoul Restaurant looked like a bowl of rice. "She looks like rice to me." b laughed at that. The smell of cinnamon was getting stronger. I started to cry. Music played from somewhere. I didn't know the song. *Life is a mystery. Everyone must stand alone.* "It's Madonna," a stranger said to me. He was one of the kids who had been next to the girl who spat on me. I nodded. He wiped away my tears. "I'm not crying because of the smoke. I'm crying because the song is so good." "I'm crying because of the smoke," b said. "I'm dizzy," I said.

Just like a prayer, you know I'll take you there. Madonna sang. Just like a prayer.

And then the whole place went silent. All I could hear was Madonna's voice. All of a sudden, I wanted to pray.

Yes, I prayed.

The ocean appeared before me: *I want to become the ocean.* That was my prayer. The way Book wanted to be a book and b wanted to be a fish, I wanted to be the ocean. But it was impossible, which is why I prayed. More and more people swarmed into the room. They danced crazily to the music. b was no longer with me. I called her in a loud voice, but all I could hear was music and the people's heavy breathing. Finally I spotted her, drifting further and further away amid all the people. She was waving at me. Then, in an instant, she was totally gone. I was surrounded by complete strangers who had no interest in me. I closed my eyes tight and the ocean appeared again. The bright blue ocean was in front of me. I tried to open my eyes. I felt dizzy. The smell of cinnamon, the music, the people and their sweat and tears made me dizzy. The owner of Alone had his arms wrapped around the girl from Seoul Restaurant. She was wearing a short skirt and swaying her hips. The floor was covered with torn-up ramyeon packages. They were torn into tiny pieces. Toothpaste caps flew over my head. Crumpled-up cigarette packs, club fliers, rocket-shaped key chains with the name of the restaurant *Seoul Restaurant*, and the phone number beneath, *8 1 6 7 1 5 5 3*, burned sticks of cinnamon and used chopsticks, and ramyeon flavoring… Suddenly people were throwing the flavoring into the fire. The whole place was filled with red-hot smoke. To lose their minds, no, because they were already out of their minds, they started to burn a plastic elephant. And a watch, a checked scarf that had washed up on the shore, a jacket with the factory's name on it, a sock, an empty pen. Now everyone's eyes were red and they shook their hips and tears ran down their faces. They shimmied their arms and their, uh, chests. They whipped their hair and made animal noises. They stretched out their arms, swung their hips, rolled their feet, and cried. I couldn't resist but stretched my arms out too, and someone grabbed onto my hand. Then someone else grabbed the other. I shook those clasped hands and yelled, "I want to be the ocean!" Then someone else yelled, "I want to die!" "No, I don't want to die. I want to be the sea!" "I want to die!" *Life is a mystery.* "But I want to die!" *Everyone must stand alone.* "But I want to die!" *I hear you call my name.* "But I want to die! I want! To die!" People yelled. All together they shouted that they wanted to die. The sound grew louder. I couldn't hear the music anymore. All I could hear was the cry: I want to die, I want to die. *But I want to be the sea!* And when I opened my eyes, miraculously, I saw Book. He was smiling. I smiled too. Smiling, I reached out to him. He reached out to me too. I started walking toward him, but then froze. He wasn't alone. Next to him was someone I knew very well. Someone who wore a hat with *Washington* written on it.

28

Washington Hat was smiling.

It was still really cute.

29

A hat, no, a few hats, smiled and reached out their tanned arms to me. Book's eyes were wide with surprise, and then he disappeared from my sight. I screamed for help, but no one could hear me amid all the cries for death. b was nowhere. I closed my eyes again, but the ocean didn't come back. Nothing came into my mind. Big hands grabbed my body tightly. And finally, Washington Hat's hand grabbed my throat.

30

"I was bored without you," said Washington Hat before kicking me. "I was really bored without you." He kicked me again. "Really bored! Did you know that?" A giant fan was spinning rapidly above me. I closed my eyes, but I could still see it. Its blades were coming closer and closer, spinning faster and faster. They would soon rip my body to pieces.

"I hate being bored," said Washington Hat. "But you made me bored."

I thought: *There's no way I can be the ocean.* And then I lost consciousness.

31

When I opened my eyes, I was in the area with the dumpsters behind the hospital. b was lying next to me. "Why did you do that?" Washington Hat was saying to Book. I could see Washington Hat. He was standing over Book, who was on the ground. The other hats were in a circle around them. Washington Hat kicked Book. "You should mind your own business. You should've kept walking." Wearing a very nice tracksuit, and smiling a very cute smile, Washington Hat kept kicking Book. Book calmly received the kicks. His body rolled from side to side on the ground. His eyes were closed and there was no expression on his face. I whispered to b, but b didn't respond. I got up. I could hear Washington Hat kick Book again and again. That's all I could hear. My head felt like it was going to shatter. Time seemed to go by very slowly, like it wasn't going by at all. Washington Hat kicked Book again. Suddenly, I saw something shiny. It wasn't a star or dust. It was a huge black rock. I picked it up. I held it tight, as though I might shatter it. Time had stopped completely. I started walking. There was the very faint sound of plastic rolling around in my sore head.

There was a thumping noise.

Then there was silence and everything stood still. Washington Hat was sprawled on the ground with a hand to his head. On the head of Washington Hat who was sprawled on the ground, instead of his hat, was something red. When I looked around the other hats, all the other hats, were staring at me. I looked at the rock in my hand. It had the same thing on it that was on Washington Hat's head. The rock fell to the ground first, and then so did I.

The End

The ocean was always the same.

*The waves lapped from left to right,
then from the left again.*

And dark, tanned boys jumped into the ocean.

1

In my dream, Book was always burning books.

2

I stared into the mirror for a long time. My reflection showed me in a school uniform. I looked really awkward. Then my mom drove me to school.

The noisy classroom hushed when I entered. Glasses was sitting in the front row. Sky sat next to him, solving problems in a workbook. I sat down behind Glasses and stared at the blackboard.

The classroom slowly grew noisier again. Except I didn't.

The bell rang.

First period was English. I took out my textbook.

The bell rang again. It was break.

The bell rang again. PE.

The bell rang again.

The bell rang again.

The bell rang again.

Each time, I took out some textbooks, put them back in my desk, went to the bathroom, or changed in or out of my gym uniform. Nobody spoke to me at all. I did everything alone. I sat, staring at the blackboard.

During lunch, I took a nap instead of eating. My dream, as always, was about Book. Book burning books, then walking into the flames. I just watched him. I didn't shout or cry. That was it—always the same dream.

"Rang Hong." My teacher was calling me.

"Yes."

"Come up here and solve question number eight." I went to the board and stared at the problem with a pen in my hand. I just stood and stared for a long time. My teacher told me to return to my seat.

The bell rang again.

I closed my bag and got up.

On the bus ride home, the girl sitting next to me whispered into her phone: *That crazy bitch is sitting next to me.* I didn't look at her. Instead, I stared out the window for a few moments, then closed my eyes.

I didn't ride the bus after that. I walked.

3

Over break, b, me, and Washington Hat were all in the same hospital. But we didn't ever run into Washington Hat for some reason. Glasses visited us exactly one time.

We went to the pork cutlet place in front of the hospital and ate pork cutlets. No one said a word as we ate.

b and I were in the same hospital room, but we didn't talk to each other. My mom didn't talk to b, and I didn't talk to her parents. We just watched television or pretended to sleep.

We were still on break when we got out of the hospital. I didn't go to the ocean; my mom wouldn't let me. Instead, I played in my grandma's room. I read the same comic book a hundred times and listened to the radio.

I went to the police station once when Book was there; the owner of Alone was with him. Book pretended like he didn't recognize me. The police called him Mister Osung Kim. *Mister Osung Kim, are you going to give us proper answers, Mister Osung Kim?* That's what they said. Book just said that he wanted a book to read. The police tossed him a sports magazine. He treated it as though it were a valuable gift. *Mister Osung Kim, you'll like prison. You'll get to read all day.* Book looked terrified. *If you don't want that, just tell us the truth!* The police yelled, and Book looked even more terrified.

"Why does Book have to go to jail?" I asked my mom.

"He won't go to jail," my mom replied.

"Then why are the police threatening him?"

Instead of answering me, she stroked my hair. I held her hand tight.

b, in the bed next to me, was alone. Her mom was in a taxi, on her way from the factory.

It always took a long time for her mom to arrive. She looked very old.

4

Book wasn't able to return to his northern hill. Washington Hat transferred schools. There was a funeral for b's sister. And then b moved away. Alone shut down. A convenience store took its place.

At school, Tokyo Hat was the new Washington Hat. Fortunately, Tokyo Hat only bullied boys. I saw Washington Hat just once more, downtown. He didn't wear a hat anymore, but had grown his hair out and dyed it blond.

Everything seemed like before. It became winter and nothing happened. Nothing kept happening. At first, I was very angry, but my anger grew smaller and eventually disappeared. Then the school year was over and then it was spring. Summer returned. Fall returned. I became an upperclassman.

I started to go to tutoring after school.

Once in a while, I would wonder where my anger had gone.

Sometimes I still went to the ocean. The ocean was always the same. The waves lapped from left to right, then from the left again. And dark, tanned boys jumped into the ocean. But I no longer wanted to become the ocean. The seasons, and the years changed. Everything was the same. After summer was fall, and after winter wasn't winter. In the end, there was no miracle. And I didn't hope for one anymore. Nothing was good anymore. The only thing left to do was turn into an adult.

I just waited to turn into an adult.